"Truly remarkable… Tanya~ ~~~~~~~~ ~~~~~~~
narrative that both sounds and feel~ ~ ~~~~~
It's like Cormac McCarthy for kids – brilliant."

Venue

"I think this novel is a masterpiece. It stands head
and shoulders above most current writing for children, and merits all the prizes for which it may be
eligible… It deserves to become a modern children's
classic."

Books for Keeps

"This challenging novel presents the often tragic
story of a remarkable woman – Siki – as she and her
tribe struggle for freedom and independence."

Robert Dunbar, *The Irish Times*

"The story is absolutely gripping and challenging. I
recommend it to any reader aged thirteen or above."

Sunday Express

"Authentic and vivid portrait of a nineteenth-century
Native American girl and her tribe's struggle for
survival."

Publishing News

"It has a strong and appealing central character, an
authentic and extraordinary setting, and a powerful
and engaging narrative."

The Sch

Apache

TANYA LANDMAN

WALKER BOOKS

First published 2007 by Walker Books Ltd
87 Vauxhall Walk, London SE11 5HJ

4 6 8 10 9 7 5

Text © 2007 Tanya Landman
Cover photograph: *Hattie Tom, Apache* by F. A. Rinehart
© Denver Public Library, Western History Collection

Extract p. 7 from *Indeh: An Apache Odyssey* by Eve Ball
published by the University of Oklahoma Press, 1988

The right of Tanya Landman to be identified as author of this work
has been asserted by her in accordance with the Copyright, Designs
and Patents Act 1988

This book has been typeset in Cochin and ATVisigoth

Printed and bound in Great Britain by
Clays Ltd, St Ives plc

British Library Cataloguing in Publication Data:
a catalogue record for this book
is available from the British Library

ISBN 978-1-4063-0331-5

www.walkerbooks.co.uk

FSC
Mixed Sources
Product group from well-managed
forests and other controlled sources
Cert no. SGS - COC - 2061
www.fsc.org
© 1996 Forest Stewardship Council

*This book is dedicated to the heroes of
the Apache nations who inspired it*

Nobody ever captured Geronimo.
I know. I was with him.
Anyway, who can capture the wind?

Kanseah

He was in his fourth summer when the Mexicans rode against us.

Tazhi, my brother: the child who delighted the hearts of all who looked upon him. The wind flowed in his veins, and the sun itself seemed to shine through his eyes when he smiled.

Only Tazhi stood and faced them.

And for that, he was cut down. In a flash of reddening steel, Tazhi was sent to the afterlife, condemned to walk for ever headless, and alone.

We were orphans of the Black Mountain Apache, Tazhi and I. Our mother had been slain by Mexican soldiers when Tazhi was a babe of ten moons old. Our father had gone from us two winters before that. He had ridden with warriors on a raid into

Mexico; there they had been ambushed. Our father was one of many who did not return.

So Tazhi and I belonged to no one, and thus we belonged to everyone – or Tazhi did.

When he was small, he had no mother to embrace him, so all the women of the tribe cuddled him, squeezing his plump limbs and tickling him until his laughs rang through the camp. As he grew bigger, he had no father to grapple and fight, so all the warriors wrestled him, delighting in his growing strength and fearless bravado. Golahka, that powerful young warrior, would play with Tazhi, although he had three children of his own. And slender Tehineh, Golahka's tender-hearted wife, would smile and look on quietly as she knelt beside the fire.

But it was I Tazhi turned to at night; I who held him through the long, black time when the coyote cried and the owl called. Tazhi would shut his eyes only when his head rested on my shoulder, and I would curl around his sleeping body to protect him from the unseen terrors of the dark.

We were at peace that summer, and happy to be so. The Mexican, it seemed, had tired of his endless war against my people, and instead had invited us to trade. Thus the whole tribe left the settlement of tepees in our Black Mountain home and for many days travelled south across the flat plains, deep into Mexican territory. Tazhi and I moved lightly, our hearts untroubled, our spirits soaring with delight to be roaming free across the land created by Ussen, the Life Giver, for the Apache.

Each night of our long journey we made camp, sleeping wrapped in blankets beneath the stars. By firelight, the old men of the tribe told tales, and Tazhi and I listened with eyes wide as they recounted how – many lifetimes ago – strangers who spoke the Spanish tongue had come from the south, butchering every tribe they met and putting whole settlements to the flame. Those they did not murder, they enslaved.

The Apache had held their freedom by moving high into the mountains where the strangers dared not venture. They kept themselves apart, and safe. But, in time, these Spanish men mingled their blood with those few of other tribes who survived their slaughter. Thus a new race was born: the Mexican, who now squatted greedily on Ussen's land and called it his own.

Conflict between the Apache and this murderous race was woven through our history like a red thread through a blanket. But now the blanket was folded and put away; there was to be no more warfare or bloodshed.

* * *

At last we stopped outside the Mexican town we call Koskineh. There Tazhi and I sniffed the air; the faint scent of cooking spices drifting from the dwellings thrilled us with its strangeness.

In the dip of a broad, open valley, where the river ran cool and clear, our tribe bent saplings and cut brushwood to fashion into wickiup shelters. We gathered wood and built fires, setting pots of meat bubbling in the flames.

For some days all was calm. In the mornings, the warriors went to trade in the town, leaving behind a small guard for the protection of the women and children.

I was then in my fourteenth summer, and was counted a woman. In the absence of my own mother, Nahasgah – mother of Golahka – had been trying to teach me the skills of womanhood that I should have mastered many, many moons ago. I had no aptitude for the tasks she set me. My fingers were clumsy when they attempted to coil baskets, and stupidly awkward when they tried to tan a deerskin. I could not scrape free the hair without nicking the outer surface, and thus each hide I worked became worthless.

To make weapons was a different thing. As soon as Tazhi could walk, I had fashioned him a small bow and a quiver full of arrows. Other boys played with sharpened sticks, but for Tazhi I made arrowheads of stone, the flint shaping easily beneath my fingers.

On our third day outside Koskineh I made Tazhi a spear.

It was not the full length of a grown warrior's lance, and yet it was no plaything. The weapon stood taller than Tazhi, but was well weighted so he could thrust it with ease. The head was long and slender, crafted from a dark flint, as sharp as the blade of the knife that all Apache carry. The shaft I had decorated with an eagle's feathers; I had found them on our journey, lying on the ground before me, as though a gift from the bird above.

When the warriors returned from trading that night, Tazhi, armed with his new weapon, barred their way. He singled out Golahka, shaking his spear threateningly, vowing to slay the warrior if he took another step.

Golahka's dark eyes glinted with seeming terror as he held his hands up placatingly. Tazhi drove him back, ordering, "Away, miserable coyote! Away from my women! Away from my children! Away, away!" And Golahka fled from the camp, screaming like a maiden.

There was much laughter amongst the women and warriors, and Tehineh smiled. Tazhi did not.

In his fourth summer, he stood proud as a mighty warrior, believing in his victory.

Chodini, chief of the Black Mountain Apache, turned to my brother and said, "We shall ride together, you and I. The earth will turn red with the blood of our enemies."

He looked at the weapon, feeling the sharpness of the flint, and gave me the briefest of nods. I flushed with pride.

But then Tehineh whispered to me, "Tazhi is indeed brave, but someone must also teach him cunning. Courage alone will not make him a warrior."

I did not think her words would come to haunt me so soon.

At sunrise the next morning, the warriors set forth once more to trade with the Mexicans, carrying with them many hides and moccasins, and beaded pouches that had been stitched during the months of winter. They also carried baskets, for the craft of the Apache women is skilled and greatly valued.

Tazhi took his spear and busied himself amongst the wickiups, learning his weapon's weight and judging how to thrust it accurately at a target. More than one dog that day learnt to run quickly when Tazhi approached.

Nahasgah called me to her, and once more began the unending task of teaching me to be a woman.

The day before, she had shown me how to coil a jug and rub the surface with red ochre to make the vessel pleasing to the eye. The whole I had then swabbed with melted piñon rosin until it was water-tight. Now the rosin had cooled and hardened, but my wretched attempt was a poor, lopsided thing.

I handed the jug to Nahasgah for her inspection. Silently she stared at it, turning my lumpen creation over in her gnarled, age-worn hands, fighting a smile that had begun to crease the corners of her mouth. After some time she said, "Take it to the river and fill it. The water you bring back will be your day's supply."

I knew I would go thirsty that day. As I walked through the grass, sunlight glinted through the gaps in my useless vessel. It would barely hold a mouthful of water – and that, only if I was lucky.

When I reached the river that skirted our camp, I dipped my jug, and sure enough the water spilt through a thousand holes. I stood it on a stone and knelt, cupping my hands in the water and lowering my face to them. I thought to have a long, cooling drink before I returned. But the sun was so warm, the day so beautiful, that I did not go back to Nahasgah at once. Instead I postponed the inevitable scolding. Trees grew either side of the river, and I had a sudden urge to climb. I craved a moment's freedom – a moment's solitude.

I swung into the branches of a pine tree – it seemed to lower itself to greet me – and climbed, the tree's spirit singing beneath my moccasined feet as they pressed against the rough bark. At last I sat high amongst the sharply scented, needle-thin leaves. A breeze rocked me in the clear air. Ussen had gifted me with the eyesight of a hawk; and in truth, sitting there, I felt as free as the eagle who soars above the plains.

Far below me, the whole camp stretched away across the broad valley. Tehineh had settled her baby upon a Mexican blanket of red and black for which Golahka had traded a basket the day before. She was quietly engaged in the many different tasks that demanded her attention: tending her fire, stirring a cooking pot, seeming at the same time to stitch a waist pouch without ever taking her eyes from her baby, or the small daughter who played at her feet. Around her, women chattered and scolded and shouted as they prepared food, stitched hides and beaded the knee-high moccasins of the Apache. Nahasgah sat twining a basket, her black eyes darting restlessly about as she watched children running between the wickiups in a frantic game of chase.

And where was Tazhi?

There!

Hunting Golahka's eldest boy, creeping towards him unseen, his spear held ready to thrust.

And then in the distance I saw a cloud of dust – the kind thrown up by the hooves of many horses. I did not call out. The warriors guarding our camp stood to see who approached, but I was not alarmed: we had been invited to this place. We were at peace. I thought they stood from curiosity, nothing more.

Some way from the camp, the leading rider raised his hand, and all came to a halt behind him. The men were dressed in the same dark clothing. Mexican troops. Still I did not sense danger.

But then – across that great distance – I heard the soft slide of metal against metal. The leader's hand had gone to the hilt of his sword. Chill horror swept through me. With a cry of sudden fear, I looked at our guards. There were but two warriors left to defend the tribe: Naneneh and Kaise, both so swift they could let fly seven arrows before the first had hit its mark. They were already taking aim.

A soft, metallic click, then a thunderous *crack!* Another! The still valley air was rent in two. And before they had loosed a single arrow, Naneneh and Kaise fell to the ground.

I looked back at the riders and saw that one held a smoking pole of metal – no longer than Tazhi's spear – in his hands. Beside him, another soldier clasped a similar length of iron. I feared it was dark magic. I had never seen a warrior slain from such a distance; never smelt the acrid tang of gunpowder; never seen a gun.

A cry of command pierced the dreadful silence. The Mexican force raised their swords and spurred their horses forward. They were galloping into our camp – stampeding through it with the rage of battle, smashing our provisions, shattering wickiups, ripping hides. Our people ran. It is the Apache way. In the face of overwhelming force: run, dodge, evade, hide. Escape. Survive. Then regroup, and on a better day fight once more.

Nahasgah fled on her aged legs, her water jug clutched in a gnarled hand as if it contained her life itself. She was felled like brushwood by a Mexican sword.

Tehineh lifted her baby from the blanket, then seized her small daughter's hand and ran. If she had thought only to save herself she would have escaped – Tehineh could run with the swiftness of the wind, and vanish into the land as if Ussen had drawn her into the clouds. But she paused, desperately looking for her son. A shot ripped first through the babe on her hip then lodged itself in Tehineh's tender heart. Blood bloomed on her deerskin shirt – sudden scarlet – like the desert flower. Her children were hacked to pieces.

And then there was Tazhi, standing motionless in the middle of the camp, his spear raised. He did not run. No one had taught him cunning. He stood and faced the Mexican force, as he had faced Golahka in play the day before. Above the noise and the screaming I could hear his high-pitched, furious shout: "Away, miserable coyotes! Away from my women! Away from my children! Away from my tribe! Away, away!"

He did not hear me call.

It happened with the swiftness of a striking snake. A Mexican with a moustache waxed sharp as the points of an arrow pulled up his horse in front of Tazhi so hard that the animal reared, its hooves flailing close to my brother's dark head. The Mexican's sword was reddened with the blood of my people; his eyes gleamed with the thrill.

Terror dizzied me; I was faint with it. I clung to the tree to stop myself falling.

Tazhi did not move. He did not take one step. He pointed his spear as if he were invincible.

The Mexican smiled upon my brother. He laughed aloud at this infant bravado.

And then he lifted his sword.

* * *

It was a long time later that our warriors returned from trading. A long time that I sat and swayed in the wind, my forehead pressed so hard against the rough bark of the pine tree that it drew blood. I did not feel it. For in that long, dead time I slipped into another place: a place of chill, numbing cold, where no pain could reach me.

And then in the soft darkness I heard the cry of a bird: the signal of Chodini, our chief. The warriors, and the women and children who had fled the Mexicans, crept quietly back into the camp.

We could not even bury our dead. We were asked to leave by our chief, silently, and at once.

I took the spear from Tazhi's stiff hand. "I will find him," I promised. "One day, little brother, I will plunge this spear into the heart of the man who killed you. You shall be avenged."

And then I left Tazhi slain upon the ground for the dogs and birds to pick at.

Through that long night's walk I said nothing. All words had withered and died within me. Even had they flowed, to whom could I have spoken? In the space of five summers the Mexican had deprived me of all: father, mother, brother. I was entirely alone.

And yet not so.

For when I had sat – head pressed hard to the pine, eyes shut against the horror spread below me – a face had formed in the darkness beneath my eyelids. Black eyes had gazed unblinking into mine, holding me still, stopping me falling.

For that long, dead time I swayed in the wind, I had looked into the eyes of my father.

I did not weep for Tazhi.

I had cried for my father when he did not return, sobbing against my mother's breast as the certainty of his death settled heavy upon us. When my mother was killed my tears had run without ceasing for a day and a night, until Tehineh had taken me in her arms and urged me to be strong, to have a heart of oak, for my brother's sake.

Perhaps I had no tears left. Through that long night's march I found that I could not weep. Grief lodged in my chest, jarring against my ribs as sharp and hard as the head of Tazhi's spear. And above and below the grief – wrapping it as the fire enfolds the log – the need for revenge burned like a cold, dark flame.

We walked in silence. There were near seventy warriors amongst our tribe. The Mexicans had numbered more than two hundred. Against such a force we could not fight. Not yet. We were deep within the land of our enemy. They had taken our horses, our weapons, our food. If they attacked again we could not hope to survive. But one day we would take our revenge. And when that day came, I swore before Ussen, I would be there to see it.

I walked alone. Behind me, so far distant that I could barely hear his soft footfall, walked Golahka. Pain swelled within my chest, making each breath hard and sharp. But even in the depth of my sadness, I could feel how mountainous a burden of sorrow he laboured under. He had lost all in one swift strike: mother, wife, son, daughter, babe. I did not wonder that he limped so far behind: I wondered that he walked at all.

At sunrise we stopped. The warriors went forth to kill what game they could, while some women lit small fires, twirling a stick between their palms until the wood beneath began to smoke. Embers were then shared with others, but my fingers were clumsy and numb. I had to sit, helpless, and watch while others worked.

When we ate, the wife of Naneneh came to me, her cheeks wet with tears. She sat beside me, cutting small hunks of meat and offering them to me on her knife. The meat tasted sour in my mouth, and my bile rose against it when I tried to swallow. She was as patient with me as with her own babe, nodding with encouragement when I forced the food down. It gave me fresh strength, and I should have been glad of her care. But when she put her hand on mine, hoping to give me comfort, I stood and walked away. I wanted no woman's softness. No purpose would be served if I broke down into weeping and wailing. My pain could not be soothed away. I did not want comfort; I wanted blood.

All this time, Golahka spoke not. He made no move to kill game with the other warriors. He ate nothing. He sat apart, and looked upon the rising sun with the eyes of a dead man.

We paused only long enough to cook and eat. There was to be sleep for none, and in truth I was glad, for how could I sleep, feeling the absence of Tazhi's small body beside me? As soon as we had finished, we marched on once more. All knew that the Mexicans might be on our trail, and that they were armed and on horseback. We were on foot; to survive, we must keep moving.

Thus we continued for two days and three nights. Hatred urged me forward and compelled me to put one moccasin before the other, until, bone-weary, we reached the southern edge of the Chokenne mountains. In this vast range of high cliffs and deep chasms we were safe. Although the Mexican claimed this land as his own, no farmer had settled this far north, and no soldier would follow where every rock, every tree, might conceal an Apache waiting in ambush.

At last, in a gully that ran into the heart of the mountains, we made camp. Here we could rest, and sleep. And here, at last, Golahka spoke.

I saw him moving amongst the warriors, talking softly to those whose loved ones lay dead. He exchanged a word here, a muttered greeting there. Then he came to me, squatting on his haunches beside where I sat in the dust, clutching Tazhi's spear. In a voice hoarse and cracked with lack of use, he spoke my name. "Siki."

He did not say more, for what more could be said? Our eyes met once. In his face was etched a loss that was past enduring. The sight of it blistered my eyes, and I lowered them to the ground. Golahka's jaw was clenched tight. He ached for vengeance. I was certain that the Mexicans would rue the day they had made him their enemy. With each heartbeat his desire for blood grew stronger. My own heart thudded in response.

After a long silence, Golahka spoke once more.

"You saw them?"

"I saw them."

"You would know them again?"

"I would."

Golahka asked me further questions, seeking to learn the colour of their clothing, and all else I could recall. From this, he could discern from which town they had set forth so he would know where to direct his attack when the time came.

"I will avenge them all," Golahka promised, standing once more. "I will slay ten Mexicans for each of our tribe. For your brother, Siki, I will slay twenty."

I shook my head.

Golahka frowned and his voice quivered with sudden rage. "Do you doubt it?"

"No," I answered, staring at the dust, wondering how I had the courage to address the mighty warrior so. "I do not doubt it. I know the rivers will run red before your thirst is satisfied. But *you* will not avenge my brother." I stood, and lifted my eyes to his. "I will."

For a brief moment Golahka's sorrow-dulled eyes blazed, then he gave the smallest of nods and was gone.

For two days we rested. The tribe ate, but talked little. Many slept; but sleep would not come to me during the long, dark nights. Grief gnawed at my soul and gave me no respite. I curled around the cold, dark place where Tazhi had once lain. The aching

wound of his absence could not be eased. Weary I
was – desperately weary – and yet I could not be still
either. I was glad when we moved once more.

Some days later, we entered our own Black
Mountains, and arrived back at our settlement.

It was a bitter homecoming.

It is the custom of our people to burn the posses-
sions of the dead.

And thus I burned our tepee, for I could scarce
bear to look upon the dusty fingermarks that Tazhi
had left on its sides. I placed his playthings in the
flames – the small bow and arrows I had once fashioned for him – and watched as they crumbled into
ashes. The tiny moccasins Tehineh had sewn and
beaded – that had filled Tazhi with such delight that
he had stared at his feet with fascination as he took
his first tottering steps, and had thus fallen headlong
into the dirt – these I threw into the heart of the
flames.

I did not burn his spear.

I watched as the fire consumed all that remained
of my brother. Fingering the sharp spearhead, I
recalled how the stone had chipped and formed
with such ease beneath my hands. I could not coil
baskets as other girls did, yet I could fashion fine
weapons. It seemed that my fingers already knew

what my mind had only just begun to realize: my destiny was not amongst the women.

I must follow the path of the warrior.

It was in the moon of many berries that we returned to our Black Mountain home. In but two moons more, winter would be upon us. Our people were without provisions; and all, according to their age and gender, set about the task of gathering food for the lean days that stretched before us.

Thus, at the sunrise that followed a night of many fires and many tears, Chodini prepared to lead his finest warriors, Golahka the first amongst them, into the land of the Mexican, where they might find horses and cattle. Others would stay behind to hunt the deer. The women and young children readied themselves to set forth and pick such nuts and berries as had ripened in our absence.

Dahtet, a woman of some fifteen summers, in whose family's tepee I had lain through the long night, held out a basket towards me and said with a gentle smile, "Come, Siki. We shall gather berries, side by side, as sisters."

I said nothing. I had told no one of my decision. But when the men assembled for the hunt, I silently took my place amongst them. I stood, chin high, challenging any to speak against me. The women cast furtive glances towards Chodini. Our chief saw where I stood, holding Tazhi's spear stiffly by my side. He looked at me for a long time, before he turned back to his warriors, but he said not a word. He did not deny my choice.

Keste, an impatient youth of some seventeen summers, not yet a warrior but who burned with the desperate desire to be so, crossed hastily to Chodini. I did not hear his muttered words, but saw him gesture angrily in my direction. Keste was known to be a fine hunter; many would heed his judgement. Yet Chodini shook his head, and when Keste persisted in his protest, our chief laid a hand upon his shoulder to silence him.

"Siki will join the hunt," he said in a calm, low voice that carried clearly to all in the camp, and admitted no further argument.

And so, that day, I took my first step on the path of the warrior.

When Ussen created each tribe, he also made their homeland, putting upon the earth all that was needed for their well-being. He set forth creatures to run upon the plains, and made such plants to grow as would provide grain and nuts and fruit. There were herbs too, and he showed the Apache how to use them to heal the sick. All that was needed for food and shelter and clothing he placed in their land.

As I walked upon the earth that morning, I felt a rising joy in my heart. I suffered still, and yet it was a soothing balm to return to my homeland. My soul, which had withered into a small, shrunken thing on the long walk from Koskineh, now expanded within me as I drew in the sweet, familiar air; for this land fed my spirit as surely as it would feed my body. The earth, my mother, seemed to set the grass singing beneath my feet as she welcomed back her people.

Softly, silently, we tracked the movement of the deer across the broad plain until at last we had sight of them in the far distance. We edged towards the herd with the wind in our faces, crawling upon our bellies, advancing one thumb's breadth at a time, carrying brushwood before us so the animals would not see our approach. I had not hunted deer before, but in truth the skills I used that day were ones I had known and practised for many summers. While my parents lived I had, in jest, spent much time creeping upon my belly that I might approach my playmates unseen, and startle them into shrieking with fear. As we came nearer to the herd I thrilled with the thought that I could make a fine hunter.

But I had not yet tried my aim. I had with me Tazhi's spear and my knife. I knew the spear to be well crafted; the head was sharp, and would penetrate the flesh of a deer easily if it were used well. But had I the skill? I did not know.

My heart began to pound as I crept towards a small doe. I sensed the excitement of the hunters either side of me as they poised to attack. Suddenly there was the soft hiss of a bowstring and an arrow flew forth, striking into the heart of the first deer with barely a sound. It was so stealthily done by Keste that the rest of the herd did not even raise their heads but continued to graze, not seeing that one of their number lay slain.

And then I cursed my stupidity. I carried naught but a spear. A spear! I could not use it from where I lay. I was not close enough. And if I were I would need to be upright, so I could draw back my arm and thrust the weapon; yet if I stood, the herd would scatter and be lost to us.

In my eagerness to join the hunters I had not seen that they carried bows – yet this was something I had known since I was an infant! My determination to become a warrior had blotted all sense – all wisdom – from my mind. I lay motionless in the grass and my cheeks flushed hot with anger and shame. How all would laugh at my simplicity! Chodini had seen how

I had armed myself – did he intend I should be the cause of my own humiliation? Had he said thus to Keste? As I cursed myself, I heard the soft swish of more bowstrings and two more beasts fell to the earth.

But now the herd sensed danger. The doe close to me lifted her head and, scenting the air, gathered herself for flight. If she ran, the rest of the herd would follow; in an instant they would be gone.

And so I acted.

A spear is for thrusting, not throwing. But in one quick movement I drew myself back on my haunches and hurled Tazhi's weapon. It pierced the doe's shoulder, sinking deep into her flesh. She was badly wounded, but she was not slain. She ran.

I do not know what I was thinking. In truth, it was surely of nothing but the spear. The doe ran with my spear. Tazhi's spear. I could not break my vow; I could not lose it.

And so I ran too.

I had always been fleet of foot – in the many races of my childhood I bested my playmates often – but a deer will always be swifter than the swiftest Apache. Yet this deer was injured; blood flowed freely from her shoulder. She dodged from side to side, and I dodged with her.

And then I drew level. To mount a running horse, I would have first grasped its mane. The doe had no mane to cling to, and so I grasped the shaft of Tazhi's spear and vaulted onto her back. My weight brought her down. Yet even now she struggled and kicked for life.

I drew my knife and thrust it into her throat, severing her vessels with my blade. She lay still. As I watched, her eyes emptied of life. She had fled into the world of the spirits. Silently giving thanks, I stood.

I had run some way with the doe. In the distance stood the men and boys of the hunt; they were looking upon me with amazement.

And so Tazhi's spear had its first taste of blood. As I pulled it from the warm shoulder of the doe and wiped it upon the prairie grass, I knew it would not be the last.

When I reached the hunters, no one spoke. At last Jotah, father of Huten, a boy who had once been playmate to me, said, "Four deer. It is a good number for one hunt."

Many nodded, for the number four is sacred to the Apache.

Then his face creased into a broad smile. "I have never seen a deer hunt that ended thus." His laughter broke the taut hush that had fallen on the hunters.

Keste alone did not laugh. Before I turned away, I saw him mouth words to Punte, his father, and shake his head in disgust.

We had no horses to carry our kill, and so we flayed and butchered the deer where they had fallen, wrapping the meat in their skins to form tight bundles. Chee worked with me, and our heads were close when he murmured, "It was well done, Siki. You will make a fine hunter."

Chee had been my friend in childhood. We had played together when we were small, until we were five or six summers old and boys and girls had to separate, as is our custom, and follow their own paths. But now we were together once more.

"Be careful," he said. "It was indeed an astonishing feat. But I do not think you have pleased Keste."

When I looked at Keste, slicing through flesh and bone with his knife, his mouth was a thin, tight line of fury.

As we returned, many came to greet us.

"A good hunt?" Keste's mother had a note of question to her voice when she saw her son's furrowed brow.

I heard him answer quietly, "She scattered the herd before we had done. We could have made a bigger kill, but for her. And look at the mess she has made of that one's hide. It can be used for nothing."

His remark stung me, but I held my tongue. I knew I had seen the deer startle, and that Keste – who had hunted closest to me – had seen it too. He was galled, I thought, by my success. I did not wish to sour him further with argument. Whining and complaint do not become a warrior; I would not indulge in a childish squabble.

Keste's next words were so soft that I barely caught them. Indeed, were it not for his mother's reaction, I would have thought I had misheard him.

"Chodini should not have let her go. How can we trust the child of such a father?"

I froze, and saw a troubled expression pass across the face of Keste's mother. She grasped him firmly by the arm. "Do not question the judgement of your chief," she urged. "To do so is unwise."

I heard no more. The women came to divide and prepare the meat. All the tribe would share in the kill, for all were hungry. Amongst the noisy chatter Keste turned on his heel and left. For some time I stood, frowning, and watched as deft fingers took my doe and began to cut her flesh into strips. Then I walked alone to the river, to wash the blood from my body.

Dahtet had returned from her berry picking and was at the river before me, about to fill her jug with cool, fresh water. She started, drawing in a sharp breath when she saw my bloody, begrimed state, and seemed uncertain how to speak to me. I smiled at her and said, "I am Siki, still."

She returned my smile, but then sighed. "For now you are Siki. But you will become a warrior. Shall you be like Golahka?"

"I would be proud to walk in his shadow."

Dahtet's voice saddened. "You choose a lonely path, Siki. A man may be a warrior and still be the father of children…"

She said no more, but I followed her thought and nodded. I would hold no babe in my arms. I would never walk with a child slung in a cradleboard upon my back. I would not feel the fierce joy of mother-hood. But I knew in my heart that I could watch no child of mine slaughtered as Tazhi had been. Better they were not born than risk such a fate.

There was a short silence. From the camp, I heard the laugh of Keste. I flushed hot with anger. He was telling someone of the hunt. I had no doubt that he was spreading the story of my supposed lack of prowess.

Dahtet too heard his laugh. Quietly she said, "Keste told me you scattered the herd."

And with Dahtet I could no longer hold my tongue. "He lies," I snapped. "They were poised

35

to flee. I saw the doe raise her head. Her quarters stiffened. I moved only then."

Dahtet said nothing. A liar is a contemptible creature, despised amongst the Apache; I did not lightly call Keste so. Yet I felt Dahtet did not believe me. She fingered the rim of her jug, and through the haze of my wrath I suddenly wondered why she had been talking to Keste at all; why she studied her jug so hard and would not meet my eyes. Unmarried men do not speak to the young women of the tribe. It is not permitted. Unless there is a promise … an understanding.

Suddenly I was as certain of it as if Ussen himself had spoken the words in my ear: Dahtet wished to marry Keste.

A cool chill crept down my spine. I knew not why the thought put such dread into my heart. As I stood beside the river, watching her fill her water jug, I knew my unease was not for myself. I feared for Dahtet.

While Chodini was absent with his warriors in Mexico, the women worked hard. Many set forth day after day to gather food; others undertook the long task of tanning hides. Some cut deer meat into thin strips, and dried it in the sun's fading heat before pounding it and placing it in baskets or hide

36

vessels. All these supplies were then carefully stored in cool mountain caves for the winter.

While the women worked, the older men of the tribe were content to sit and smoke and tell stories of battle feats and acts of bravery. The younger men listened, burning for the chance to be the heroes of their own tales. Wrestling matches and trials of strength were what occupied the boys. They played mock battles with each other, hurling stones with their slingshots.

And on those days I belonged with no one. The women looked sideways at me when I went to join them, as indeed they always had – at first for my ineptitude, but now for the path I followed. My love of solitude had long been curious to them, and though Nahasgah had looked tenderly upon me, and Tehineh had often called me little sister, they were gone now, and many women shrank from my strangeness. I was to be a warrior; seemingly I had exiled myself from the company of women. Yet neither did I wish to be amongst the youths of the tribe when our chief was absent, for such behaviour might be spoken of as immodest, and I did not wish to call down censure on my head.

Thus I was content to remain alone, keeping my hands and mind occupied in fashioning a bow, arrows and wrist guard that I might carry when next we hunted deer. With these, I practised my aim on frogs and fishes and creatures that crawl upon the earth, as any small boy would. As Tazhi had once done.

In those solitary days, I thought of Keste's muttered words.

My father had gone from us before my mother's belly was seen to swell with the child that was Tazhi. He left the living earth eight moons before Tazhi kicked his way into the sunlight. At his birth, my mother had wept hard, agonized sobs because my father was not there to look upon the face of his son. And yet my father had died a warrior's death. My mother had clung with pride to that. No blemish stained his reputation.

Why then had Keste spoken as if he was one disgraced?

It was near five winters since I had watched my father ride away. His beloved face had become blurred and indistinct in my memory. And yet at Koskineh, in the darkness behind my closed eyelids I had beheld every line, every curve, of his features. Strange that now – when I had seen him so clearly – Keste should speak of him.

I would have dismissed Keste's gibe as meaningless. Easy, it would have been, to have shrugged away his overheard words as mere spite, but his mother's troubled confusion gave weight to them. There was something here that I could not comprehend. Had Nahasgah or Tehineh lived I could, perhaps, have taken my questions to them. Alone, I could come no closer to understanding what he meant.

Some days later, Chodini and his warriors returned. He brought many horses and cattle to supply the needs of his tribe; a good chief will serve as well as lead his people, and it was for this reason that Chodini was so beloved. We could face the coming winter without fear of hunger.

And now Chodini called a council of the warriors.

They gathered in the grey light of dawn, each according to his rank. Ozheh, son of Chodini, sat at his father's right hand; Golahka sat at Chodini's left – the finest of his men.

I dared to approach.

I sat behind the line of the youngest warriors – those who had not yet been tried in battle. Women warriors are not unknown amongst the Apache; yet not many choose the path I now followed. Squatting in the dust beside Chee, awkwardly conscious of my strangeness, I sat with those youths who had but lately begun their training. We were permitted only to listen; none but the warriors were allowed to speak.

No one challenged me. The slightest tilt of Chodini's head gave me to understand that I was permitted to join them. I could not see the face of Keste, but my presence was like a pebble dropped into a still pool: his ill humour rippled outwards, causing Chee to raise his eyebrows and then suppress a smile. I did not doubt that Keste was my enemy, and yet I knew not what had roused him so against me.

When all had assembled, Chodini stood and addressed the council.

"My kinsmen. My brothers. All have seen what the Mexicans did to our people. All have suffered. No family has escaped without loss. All mourn loved ones."

He paused, letting his eyes rest upon Golahka, who had lost all. The warrior's face was unmoving and cold as stone.

Chodini spoke once more, his voice rich with passion. "These Mexicans are but men – mortal men – as we are. They invited us to trade in a time of peace. Then they rode against our women, our children, against those who were powerless to protect themselves. We shall repay their treachery. We shall repay it tenfold. Let us go forth and avenge this wrong!"

His voice was barely a whisper when he asked,

"My brothers, will you come?"

None were compelled to fight. It is not the Apache way for a chief to order his warriors into battle; he may lead, and they may follow, yet each man is free to make his own decision.

None refused. All were willing to take the warpath to Mexico. Each man shouted his assent, until the mountains rang with their fierce cries.

And now my heart pounded and the blood raced in my ears. It was possible that I too would return to the land of my enemy. I might be allowed to accompany and serve the warriors as a novice if I were deemed worthy. *If* I were deemed worthy. I was determined that it should be so.

Chodini invited Golahka to stand. Laying a hand upon his shoulder, our chief addressed the council once more.

"We are but few and the Mexicans are many. And yet the wrong has not been done to our tribe alone: it has been done to the whole Apache nation. Golahka shall journey to our brother tribes to ask if they will join us. He shall ride to meet the Dendhi and the Chokenne."

On hearing the word "Chokenne" my heart contracted. It is the common custom of my people that when a man marries he will join the tribe of his wife. Not all do so. But my parents had followed this tradition. My mother had been of the Black Mountain Apache, and when he took her as his bride my father had become one of Chodini's warriors. But he had been born Chokenne, and grew to manhood in their craggy mountain range that ran deep into the land the Mexicans now claimed as their own.

The warriors were nodding and calling out their approval of Chodini's choice of envoy; all were content for Golahka to go forth, for he was eloquent, and in the ways of war his prowess was unrivalled.

The warrior council dispersed. I did not move. Chee rose, but I did not go with him. When Golahka fixed me with his bleak eyes I did not flinch from his gaze, though my heart pounded hard against my ribs. Instead I sat, and waited until we two were left alone.

And then Golahka came to me and spoke. "You wish to return to Mexico?"

As I looked at him, I felt my eyes blazing with the lust for revenge. "Yes" was my only answer.

Golahka nodded. "It may be so," he said. "Indeed it may. But first you must prove yourself worthy to tread the path of the warrior."

I nodded. I knew what lay ahead. Rising to my feet, I stood silently while he spoke of what I must do.

"At dawn you must depart, alone. Follow the

mountains. Take food for seven sunrises. Speak to none but Ussen. Be with none but Ussen. Examine your heart. When I return from the Chokenne, you will know if you are worthy."

Excitement rose in my chest. Excitement – and fear. But I nodded, readily accepting my trial.

"Go then," he said. "Make your preparations."

As I turned from him, he said softly, "While you are away, do not scatter the deer."

I spun on my heel to face him. "I did not!" The words tumbled from my lips before I could stop them. Swiftly I slammed my mouth shut, biting my tongue to stop more spilling forth. In the coming days I would face worse perils than the false reports of Keste. I would not trouble Golahka with pettish quarrels.

The faintest flicker of wry amusement passed across the warrior's face. He said quietly, "I know of no boy – nor any man – who has caught a running deer. And I do not believe that any who could do as you did would have misjudged when to strike."

At that, he turned and walked away.

Small wonder that my heart became swollen with pride.

It was to Dahtet I went in search of dried meat and fat for my journey. When I made my request, it seemed I need not have wasted words in asking, for she had already packed provisions into a hide bag and filled a vessel with sweet spring water. Smiling, she handed these to me.

"Your training has begun, has it not?" she said softly. "And now you must go forth." She paused, and then murmured, "Be careful, Siki."

She said no more: she did not need to. I had known these mountains since my infancy, but I had never gone forth entirely alone. Bears roamed amongst the pines; mountain lions made their homes between the rocks. Alone, I would be small match for either beast. I felt a stab of panic.

But I had my spear – Tazhi's spear – my newly fashioned bow, a quiver full of arrows and my flint knife. They would serve me well. I could survive. I must. I thanked Dahtet, and turned to the task that faced me, thinking only of the morning.

I did not sleep: I could not.

I had always prized solitude, always cherished my stolen snatches of freedom. Yet at nightfall I had always been glad to return to the warm familiarity of my tribe. The coming nights would be long, and lonely, and I was afraid.

Seeking strength, I reached for my father; his eyes had held me firm in the tree at Koskineh and

I hoped his memory would now lend me fresh courage. But each time I grasped for his face it evaded me, slipping like water through my fingers. As the sky started to lighten I sighed, and turned my mind instead to the task that lay before me. And then – for one heartbeat – I caught a glimpse of him. An image flashed in my mind, bright as the sudden lightning that turns night to day. But he was not standing, not holding me with his gaze. This time, my father was leaning against a rock, panting, exhausted, and his eyes were wide with fear.

When the sun lit the sky with golden streaks, I heard the soft footfalls of Golahka. Then there came the hoof beats of a horse departing from the camp through the mountains towards the south, where dwelt the Chokenne Apache. Senseless it seemed to remain tossing restlessly, listening to the breathing of Dahtet's family as they slept, and thus I rose also to depart for my trial of endurance. I gathered my weapons, my food and my water vessel, and turned my face to the north.

As I left the tepee, I saw the hoof prints of Golahka's horse clear in the dust. And it was then, in my youthful pride, that I was seized by a fresh conceit. I suddenly thought to trail Golahka; to pursue him by furtive means as I had once pursued my playmates; to track him silently as I had tracked the deer.

Golahka had told me to go alone into the mountains, but he had not said into *which* range I should go. Little difference then, I reasoned, if I remained in the craggy peaks of my home, or if I followed him to the sierras where the Chokenne dwelt and where my father had grown to manhood.

My heart was filled with rushing excitement for the task I had set myself. I would trail the mighty warrior unseen into the heartland of the Chokenne; I would witness their council – with Golahka all unknowing. When he returned to question me of my trial, how startled he would be by my knowledge of his journey.

True enough, Golahka was on horseback, and I was on foot. But as I read the tracks, I could see he had not ridden fast; there was no need for him to do so – he was not pursued by enemies. To follow a man so dulled with sadness that he moved without caution or fear would be an easy task. I could do it.

I turned my face to the south, and began my journey.

The mountain ranges in the great land Ussen gave to the Apache run from north to south. It is possible to travel for many miles through the safety of the high rocks, where there is fast-flowing water, plentiful

46

game, much wood to make fire, and cover so that the hunter may move furtively, unseen by the prey he stalks. But to journey from one tribe's heartland to another, it is necessary to cross the vast plains that divide the ranges.

For the length of a day, I trailed Golahka to the very edge of the Black Mountains. On horseback, he had to follow the winding trail that zigzagged between the outcrops of stone. My path was swifter, for I was on foot and could climb sheer places where a horse could not go. Thus I kept him in sight. He reached the plain at sunset, and made his camp at the foot of the hills. In a deep arroyo where he could not be seen he lit a small fire.

Cooking vessels are fragile – fashioned from clay and easily broken. To travel carrying such a thing would be an awkward encumbrance. Thus the Apache keep many such things stored in secret caches throughout the land. I watched as Golahka broke away crusted earth and stones that sealed a small cave. Pulling out a red-baked pot, he crumbled into it a handful of the dried, pounded meat from the bag at his waist, poured on water, and set the whole in the fire to cook. The meat, I knew, would swell and yield enough to fill his belly.

It was not so for me. I did not dare to light a fire of my own. Instead I drank such sweet spring water as remained in my vessel and – with the scent of Golahka's mash filling my nostrils and making my mouth run with saliva – chewed on a strip of deer meat. The handful of berries I had gathered as I walked finished my small meal. And then I sought a place where I might try to sleep through the long night that fast approached. I would not rest under the cover of a tree, for I had known since infancy that this was the first place a wild beast – or an enemy – would search for me. Rather I settled at the foot of a rock face, that I might climb swiftly to escape if danger threatened.

Golahka had wrapped himself in his blanket, and I envied him. In my great haste, I had left my own behind in the tepee. I had no fire, no covering. Sleep did not come easily.

At dawn, Golahka began his long trek across the broad plain. I watched from the mountains as he travelled; he did not ride at speed and once more I was grateful, for my progress would be slow indeed. There was sparse cover, little that would conceal me from his view, so I had to keep low, crawling where the vegetation grew thin. Travelling thus, I could not cross the plain before evening so would have to continue my journey at night. Darkness would conceal me, and I could then move more swiftly, but

I would face new dangers, for at night snakes slide silently across the earth bringing painful death to those who walk unwary.

From my hiding place in the hills I scanned the flat land below, seeing where the patches of green growth showed the presence of water. These I fixed in my mind, for I would be in need of a drink before the day ended; and, first refilling my vessel, I began to traverse the plain.

On the third day, at sunrise, Golahka entered the mountains of the Chokenne. When he rode, I hastened forward, for there would be cover where I could follow close and remain unobserved.

For a long time I crept in the path of Golahka's horse. In these mountains I could take no shorter route, for I did not know them as well as my own. Golahka too was tracking, searching for the signs that would lead to the Chokenne.

Once, I came almost upon him. He had suddenly turned back, swinging his horse hard round and startling me. I slipped into a narrow crevice and froze, utterly motionless, until my sinews screamed and my muscles throbbed in desperation. The eye must always be drawn to movement – the smallest flicker of a bird's wing, the slow glide of a leaf dropping to the earth – and will pounce upon it as the mountain lion leaps upon the deer. I was so placed that if I moved even a hair's breadth, Golahka would know of my presence. And so I remained still.

The warrior stopped to set a fire burning, and began to eat agonizingly slowly. At last, when I thought I must give myself away, so desperate was I for movement, he rode once more.

And now in the distance I could see smoke from the Chokenne campfires rising in the evening light. In my youthful stupidity, I believed I had reached the end of my journey – that I had only to follow the direction of the smoke to come secretly upon the camp. Thus I thought to keep myself further back from Golahka; I would not risk being discovered by him or any of the Chokenne.

As the sun began to sink, I saw a small stream in a gully below me. I was thirsty, and sought to replenish my water. I needed to rest and to chew on some dried meat. When I had drunk of the clear water and eaten, I climbed back to the trail of Golahka. I came to a jutting rock and as I rounded it, I saw to my dismay that I had been mistaken.

The mountain fell away sharply before me, as steep as if Ussen himself had cut it away with his flint-sharp knife. Golahka could not have ventured down it on horseback; indeed, it would be impossible to pass that way on foot. A gaping ravine lay between myself and the camp of the Chokenne. I knew not where Golahka had gone.

I was in unknown territory, and I had lost the warrior's trail. Greatly vexed, I berated myself for my folly. I cursed aloud, the words spilling freely in the mountain air.

It was then that I felt the knife against my throat.

I was filled with such terror as I hope never to feel again.

I did not fear to die: it meant but a passing from this life to the next. There I would hunt and ride as I did upon the living earth. Death held no horror for me. But I had seen what the Mexicans did to my mother before they killed her, and I knew that there are things worse than a swift and easy death.

My mind was frozen with fear. I did not move; I made no sound. I stood still while the cold knife grew warm against my throat. And then at last the man who held me fast relaxed his grip and spun me round. I could not help myself: I shut my eyes. I did not wish to see the face of my tormentor.

It was the last time I ever showed such weakness.

Only when he spoke did I realize who had rendered me witless.

Golahka.

At once I was flooded with relief so strong that

my legs struggled to hold me; I was unsteady as a newborn deer who takes its first quaking step. And then I felt shame, burning hot, pricking my eyes with salt tears. I would not let them fall. I sank my nails into my flesh and clenched my jaw tight.

"I should leave you here for the lions and bears to prey upon," Golahka said, his voice ringing with anger. "Foolish girl! For three days you track me. Yes, I knew you followed! Why else would I ride so slow? For three days you keep well hidden. Then you forget yourself! Did you think your journey was ended? Is that why you let slip your caution?"

He spoke true: I had relaxed, and come from the stream carelessly. Worse, I had cursed aloud – aloud! – when I should have kept my silence.

"A thoughtless warrior earns nothing but a shameful death," spat Golahka. "And you – *you* – who wished to follow the warpath to Mexico, to walk in the land of our enemies! You should not have been so easily caught!" He shook his head, and said in a voice that shrivelled my spirit, "Be glad I was not a Mexican."

Shame tore at my chest sharp as a wolf's teeth. To be disgraced before any warrior would have been hard indeed to endure; but to be disgraced before Golahka – whose esteem I had longed to win – was beyond bearing. Had he ordered me to leap into the ravine before us, I would have done so; it would have been easier than suffering such humiliation.

He walked away, and the briefest jerk of his head told me to follow.

His horse was tethered along the track – the very track I had followed before I had set off to the stream. Had I kept myself alert on my return I would have seen the beast and known of Golahka's ambush, and yet I had wandered blindly into his trap. It was the end of my training. Bleakly I knew I could not now earn the title warrior – I did not deserve it. Hope vanished, as the sun behind a storm cloud, leaving only cold and darkness and freezing rain. To be shamed is bitter indeed to the Apache.

Golahka sprang upon his horse in a single bound and extended his hand for me to grasp. Clumsy in my disgrace, I scrambled, ungainly, behind him. Grunting with contempt, Golahka urged the animal forward, and we rode, by a perilous winding trail, towards the camp of the Chokenne.

It was full darkness when we came to their settlement, and the fires burned bright. The smell of cooking hung upon the night air, and yet I felt no hunger, for shame had dulled my appetite. When those of the Chokenne stood and stepped forward, I could not meet the gaze of any who came to greet us.

The great chief, Sotchez, embraced Golahka as a

brother. When the women came to claim me as their own, I did not resist. I was banished from the path I desired and with a heavy heart I knew that now my fingers must learn to coil baskets and bead moccasins.

But the anger of Golahka had softened in the warmth of the campfire.

"Do you go with the women, Siki?" he said. "Are you vanquished so easily? Do you fight no more?"

At last I lifted my eyes to look at him, and with joy I saw no rage burning there.

"No," I answered, striving to keep my voice strong and steady. "I am shamed ... shamed indeed. But not vanquished."

He nodded.

And then I found the courage to ask him, "How did you know I would follow?"

At that Golahka laughed: a loud, clear peal that rippled across the night sky and set the stars jangling. "How did I know?" he echoed. He leant forward so that his hair brushed against my own, and said in a soft voice that none but I could hear, "Because it is exactly what I would have done myself."

The Chokenne and Black Mountain Apache are brother tribes, woven together for many lifetimes with marriages and ties of blood. As I looked about me, I saw warriors whose faces I remembered from my childhood: boys from the Black Mountains who, on becoming men, had chosen women of the Chokenne for their brides and thus joined Sotchez's tribe. Goyenne, daughter of Chodini, had become wife to the great chief Sotchez many summers before. He had chosen not to leave his own people when he married, and thus Goyenne had agreed to bid farewell to the Black Mountains and join the Chokenne when she wed.

As word of the massacre at Koskineh spread around the camp, mournful cries rent the dark night. There is no sound more terrible than the Apache death wail. Those cries told of such sadness, such piercing anguish. It was hard indeed to bring our story to the ears of the Chokenne.

Goyenne embraced me, calling me sister, before drawing me aside to hear word of the slain. When I told her of the death of Golahka's family she wept salt tears, though she tried to hide them. I did not speak of Tazhi, for she had not known him, and in truth I did not want her pity: it would soften my resolve.

Sotchez called upon his warriors to meet at council when the sun rose, and then all retired to their homes to mourn their slaughtered kinsmen.

I was to stay in the tepee of a young warrior

named Pocito. "Come, sister," he said. "You are weary. Come eat, come rest, come sleep."

His wife, Denzhone, made much of me, bustling to lay out her finest hides upon which I might take my rest. Indeed, she was so busy that in her noise and haste she woke her children, who had been sleeping peacefully. The youngest was but still a babe; the eldest was a boy of perhaps four summers. His limbs had not quite lost their infant plumpness. He was the same size as Tazhi had been.

The boy looked at me, his black eyes bright with curiosity. "Mother, who is she?" he asked. "Why does she come into our home?"

Denzhone scolded him, telling him to hold his tongue, and the child asked no more questions. But deep within me, I felt the spark of curiosity smoulder and ignite.

The child had spoken slowly, and his mouth had struggled with the shapes of the words as if they did not come easily. He had frowned while his mind reached for the simple phrases he had uttered. He had spoken as if Apache was not his mother tongue.

I was curious, but that night I was also bone-weary. As soon as I lay upon the soft hides I had been offered, sleep enveloped me and I yielded to the silent darkness, considering the boy no more.

* * *

When the sun rose high above the mountains, the Chokenne warriors gathered in council.

I watched as they sat upon the ground, and bit my lip to keep inside the words that longed to spill from my mouth. My father's father and mother were long since dead. But here were the men amongst whom my father had grown to manhood. With these warriors he had played and fought when still a boy. Did any recall him? Did any see an echo of his face when they looked upon my own? I could ask no one. The Apache are loath to speak the names of the dead lest they be recalled from the afterlife and walk upon the living earth once more. I could not ask my questions, yet neither could I silence them; they goaded me as flies in the heat of summer.

Sotchez made a sign to Golahka, who stood and addressed all who had gathered to hear him.

"My brothers," he said in a voice that commanded all ears, "you know now that our people were slain at Koskineh. These were not warriors, killed honourably in battle, but women and children butchered in a time of peace. We were there to trade; we had come at the Mexicans' invitation. We were wrong to trust those vipers, for their troops came against us. Our women, our children, the warriors who sought to defend them – all paid the price of our mistake."

Golahka paused until the air ached with his silence. His voice when it came again was hard as flint.

"You all know the way of battle. You may be killed; you may return. Be certain you think of this before you make your choice. My brothers, I ask that you follow me. Avenge the wrong that has been done to our people. My kinsmen ... will you come?"

None could deny the justice of his cause. The warriors who sat upon the ground were as impatient for vengeance as I was. With fierce shouts, all agreed that they would join the Black Mountain Apache on the warpath.

"It is well," said Golahka. "I say now that all may know: if I am killed, none need mourn me. My family lies slain in Mexico. I am content to die there if need be."

"And I too," I murmured. No kin would mourn if I did not return. None would weep. No lamenting wail would pierce the sky for me if I met my end there. My only prayer to Ussen was that I would not die before Tazhi's spear had found the heart it sought.

We left the Chokenne as the sun crested the sky and began its slow descent. Sotchez promised Golahka that when the winter had passed, in the moon of fresh leaves, he would join us on the warpath to Mexico. While the two men embraced as brothers and made their farewells, I looked about me.

I was standing in the mountains where my father had played as a child. To me it seemed as though a whisper of his presence remained. If I narrowed my eyes I could almost see his boyish form wrestling with another in the dust, and my mind ran free with happy imaginings.

Pocito bade me farewell, and his wife and children came forth to see me take my leave. As I looked upon the boy I was again seized with a woman's curiosity. He spoke so slowly, so awkwardly. Sudden certainty crept across my mind.

I bent my knees, lowering my face to his level, and, smiling, spoke the one word I knew of the Spanish tongue.

"*¡Adiós!*"

It was clumsily said and sounded strange in my mouth, and yet all at once, the boy's eyes shone bright, and a babble of words streamed forth. I understood none of them.

Still smiling, I shook my head, telling him I did not speak his mother tongue. I ruffled the boy's hair, and then sprang onto the back of the horse behind Golahka in readiness to return home. My last sight of the Chokenne showed me Denzhone,

59

her hand resting upon the boy's shoulder, holding him fondly against her as if he were her true-born son. And yet I knew it could not be so. The boy they loved as their own was Mexican.

It should not have surprised me. The Mexican has always ridden against the Apache. Summer after summer, they have murdered our warriors, slaughtered our children and taken our women for slaves. When they settled upon the land made by Ussen, they filled our grassy plains with their grazing cattle and horses and drove away our game. But why should our people go hungry amid such bounty? Thus have our warriors hunted cattle and horses instead of buffalo that they may fill the empty bellies of their wives and children.

Sometimes, when a warrior returns from such a raid, he will also bring a child. Indeed, when Chodini had lately returned to our people driving many animals ahead, a small girl of no more than one summer had sat astride the horse in front of him. Chodini had given the child to a woman whose infant daughter had been butchered at Koskineh, for the girl would ease the aching void left by the babe's loss. It is the custom of our people to rear such captive children as our own. Soon the girl would be calling the Apache woman mother as if she had never known any other. Like the son of

Denzhone, the girl would become one with our people, a Mexican no more – and as precious and well beloved as Tazhi had been.

We rode but half a day before the setting sun made us halt our journey homewards, and we rode in silence. Soldiers rarely ventured into the Chokenne range, but well we knew that there were bloodied hunters amongst the Mexicans – men of dreadful skill – who sold Apache scalps for cold coin as they might sell the tanned hide of a deer. We made no fire and ate little, for our stomachs had been well filled by the hospitality of the Chokenne.

Strange it seemed to lie on the ground so near to Golahka, and my heart thudded uncomfortably with its awkwardness. Sleep was slow to claim me, and dreams, when they came, were full of Tazhi. Over and over I saw him standing in front of a horse, holding his spear as if he were invincible. Again and again, above the noise and screams, I heard his high-pitched, furious shout. I saw the Mexican, my enemy, and heard his laugh. Saw his sword swing. Red steel. And Tazhi was no more. Each time, I woke sweating, my hands balled into fists that ground against my eyes in frustration.

And then, shortly before dawn, I slipped into a different dream entirely.

I was running. Running with happy ease, my heart light and free from care. Out of my range of vision, his moccasins pounding the dry earth behind me, was my father. Often we had raced thus in my childhood; he had joyed in my fleetness of foot with a father's great pride.

We ran on, and on. But slowly, for thought comes slow and heavy in dreams, I realized something was badly amiss. He ran not in joy, but in terror. This was a wild, reckless flight. He ran with his mouth agape, his throat and tongue drying in the hot air, his breath broken and laboured. He was exhausted: his pace faltered; his steps grew uneven; he staggered. At last he collapsed, spent, beside a rock. I stopped, but in this strange dreamworld I found I could not turn to face him.

And yet I knew how he looked, for had I not seen his image flash through my mind before I began my journey to the Chokenne? I knew he stood eyes wide with fear – and now I knew the cause, for I heard the soft thud of pursuing feet. I could not see who hounded my father. My own body had grown immensely heavy; I had not the strength to move. I hung my head with weariness and stared at the ground.

And as I stared, from behind me – from where my father drew anguished breaths – came a dark stain that pooled about my feet like blood. A stain that widened and grew and spread. A stain that crept across the dry earth until it covered the plains below me, and the whole land was smothered with a vast, black shadow.

At dawn, Golahka seemed to sense my distress, for he set me a task that would stretch my mind as surely as it would my body.

"Siki," he said, "you must yet prove yourself worthy to train as a warrior. You will go now. I shall remain here until the sun is high. It is two days' journey to the camp of our people. Get there before me."

At first, I was dismayed by the simplicity of the task. But then he added, "Enter our camp on horseback."

"On horseback?" I echoed, perplexed.

Golahka knew – as did I – that there were no horses near but those of the Chokenne. If I journeyed the half-day back to their settlement I could not hope to reach our own tribe before Golahka. Even had I done so, I could not have taken a horse from our brothers, and it was doubtful indeed that they would give me one; as winter approached surely they would have none to spare, for horses provide meat when it is needed, as well as the means by which we ride.

Golahka watched me, his black eyes burning as I sought to divine his meaning.

"There are no horses…" I mumbled stupidly, my brow furrowing with confusion.

"None?" he asked. It was spoken as a question, and yet I knew it was not so. With a single word, he had explained all.

There was but one horse close by.

My eyes rested on the dark mare Golahka rode, who stood grazing beside us. When I looked back at Golahka, I at last understood his meaning. He meant me to pit my wits against his; to ambush him, as he had ambushed me; all this and yet more – he had challenged me to take from him his horse, and to ride her home before him.

It was an impossible task. He could have ordered me to pluck the sun from the wide sky, or peel the moon's image from the river, and with these two tasks I would have had, perhaps, some chance! But to outwit a warrior as famed as Golahka? It could not be done! Of this I was certain. Yet I clung to the challenge; it would absorb my whole attention and keep my mind from my troubled dreams.

And so I set forth without further word, my head buzzing with plans. So full was it, there was no room to admit any thought of my father.

* * *

I still had half a day's journey through the mountains of the Chokenne before I would reach the great plain that divided the ranges. I moved at a steady lope, a pace between a walk and a run which carries the Apache across much land in but a short time. I wanted to get far, far ahead of Golahka that I might give myself time to think, to plan how I might outwit him. As I covered the ground, I kept my eyes opened wide, observing every gully, every tree, every hiding place from which I might ambush the great warrior.

I rejected them all. Golahka, I knew, would see each place as I did. He would know at once if I was concealed. And even if he did not, what then? I could not hope to push him from his horse; my strength was not equal to his. If I dropped from a tree upon his back, I would have as much chance of toppling him as the mountain rat against the lion.

How, then, if I approached while he slept? I knew I could come upon the deer silently – could I do in like fashion against Golahka? I turned the thought in my head as I hastened through the winding mountains. Certain was I that I could approach him. But that was all. Golahka slept like the wolf, in short snatches: ever alert, ever wary. Having set this challenge, he would keep the horse hobbled – her front legs tied together – close by him, and I did not see how I could set her free and vault upon her back with not a single sound. And yet another thing decided me against this plan: it was too simple an idea; one that any who hoped to be a warrior might decide upon. Golahka would expect it. No... I must find another strategy. One that he would not anticipate. I must find a way to deceive him.

And yet, try as I might, I could not. I kept up my pace through the long, hot day. The sun was high as I reached the wide plain and this I began to cross in great haste. It was not cautious to do so – in bright daylight I could be watched by any enemy that lurked unseen. I was utterly without cover, utterly unprotected, as I ran. Yet I trusted that Ussen would keep me from danger, and in truth the task had a greater importance in my mind than my own safety.

At moonrise I walked on, not ceasing until I at last reached the foot of the Black Mountains. Here I settled, and chewed upon more of Dahtet's dried meat. Then I lay upon the dusty ground that I might refresh my body with some little sleep. Across the flat land Golahka would come at dawn, and this time I knew he would cross swiftly, meaning to reach our camp before I did.

Golahka was a proud warrior; he did not intend that I should succeed. The knowledge that this was so, that he did not think me capable of besting him, hardened my will. I would do it. I would. I wished it with such fervour that I too slept in short snatches.

In the times of wakefulness, I lay looking at the bright stars that Ussen had set in the night sky, and I prayed that an idea would come. And in the darkest moment before dawn, it did.

I hastened once more, climbing into the mountains I had known and loved since my infancy. It was now but a short distance to our camp: one day's journey through the rocky land I had known all my life. Golahka too knew the land there well. As well as I. Almost.

Golahka had been born of the Hilaneh Apache, whose territory lay to the east. His boyhood days had been spent at the headwaters of the Hila River, and not amongst these stones. He had not played in these mountains as a child. And there are places known only to children where they may hide and an adult will never think to look. Golahka's eldest boy had known of these, but Golahka did not.

There was one such hiding place: a sloping ravine whose walls were so narrow that they blocked out the sun. It began high in the last rocky outcrop before our camp, close to the path where Golahka must pass. It then declined sharply, ending at the foot of the rocks near the river where surely Golahka must pause and allow his horse to drink before riding home. Many times had I slid through this tunnel in play, delighting in the speed of my descent, but I had not ventured there since before Tazhi's death. I hoped I had not grown so much I could no longer use it.

This then was my plan: to lay a false trail and deceive the greatest of the Apache warriors. My head told me that such a thing was not possible, and yet hope tiptoed on softly moccasined feet, setting my heart beating with excitement.

I was almost within sight of our camp when I began to lay my false trail. Until then I had not troubled to cover my tracks; Golahka would see I had moved with weary urgency. If he thought I was racked with desperation and had become careless, so much the better.

There was but one path Golahka could follow upon the mare. Had he been on foot, my task would not have been so easy, but the ways a horse may pass are not so many as those a lone Apache may choose. I came to the jutting rock in the shade of which I knew lay the entrance to my tunnel. Further along the path was an overhanging tree. Here would I set my mock ambush.

I knew I would fail. I planned to. Yet Golahka must believe I had wished to succeed. And thus, in this one place, I covered my tracks. I covered them, but not so well that a skilled warrior would fail to see the small signs I had seemingly overlooked in my youthful carelessness – a broken stalk of grass, a bent twig. Signs that would tell Golahka I was hidden behind a rock beside the tree, waiting to throw him from his horse.

And what next? I could not hope to wrest him from the mare's back by strength alone. Golahka knew that as well as I. So I would have to dislodge him by other means.

It was as if Ussen himself wished to aid me. One of the tree's branches grew across the path; Golahka would lower himself onto the mare's neck to avoid it when he passed. But the branch was thin, and supple, and it was a simple task to pull it back and tie it to the rock I hid behind. As he came level with the tree, I would cut the strip of hide that held it, and the branch would spring forward and dislodge the warrior from his horse.

Such was the plan I wished Golahka to see. It could not succeed. I hoped only that he would believe I had made an earnest attempt at ambush. As I sat behind the rock awaiting his arrival, I began to feel the plan was so simple he would not believe in its sincerity. He would at once see I meant to deceive him. If he did, I would indeed fail.

Golahka had given me half a day's lead, but he had travelled swiftly behind me. I did not have half a day to wait before his horse approached, and I heard the warrior's soft, mocking laugh. He said nothing.

The mare came on but I dared not peer over the rock. As she drew level, I sliced the buckskin with my flint knife. The branch snapped back, sweeping across the path with a crack. It hit nothing. The horse walked on beneath it, and I saw she was already riderless.

At once Golahka leapt upon the rock I cowered behind, his eyes brimming with laughter.

"A fine attempt." He smiled. "But I am not ambushed."

In two short bounds, he was once more mounted upon the mare, urging her forward along the mountain track. He was laughing. He had believed in my witless attempt. And now he had relaxed his guard. He was almost within sight of our tepees; he had but to follow the winding path that led down to the valley. I could not get past him; I could do nothing to him now. Thus thought Golahka, I was certain of it. And I was as certain that I would yet prove him wrong.

Leaving my food and weapons where I knew I could find them later, I ran to the jutting rock. I squeezed beneath it, edging round to where the entrance of the tunnel lay. An adult would feel but a gap, a slit in the rock, too small to pass through. Only a child could know what was beyond. I edged into the tunnel, feeling the tightness of the stone against my sides. I began my descent through the rock that had been worn smooth by the passage of countless Black Mountain children.

But I could not glide as fast as I had once. When smaller, I had slid freely from top to bottom, where now I had to crawl, and squeeze, and force myself through gaps that did not wish to let me pass. But I was of slighter build than many of my age, and I could do it. I was slower than I had hoped. Yet when I emerged into the sunshine, I heard the hoof beats of Golahka's horse still high above me as he zigzagged his way down the path.

I went swiftly to the river, walking on stones so I would not leave tracks for Golahka to see. At the edge, I lowered myself into the cool, clear water carefully, so that I would not stir up mud and give myself away. A rock overhung the river, beside the place where Golahka and the mare would cross, and it was here I concealed myself, scarce daring to breathe in case the ripples should betray me.

Here I waited, hoping, praying, that Golahka would rest and allow his horse to drink.

Again Ussen was with me. Golahka did indeed stop. The mare lowered her head, sucking in cooling gulps but a hand's width from where I lay. And Golahka was so confident of his success, that for a moment he released his hold upon the reins and extended his arms in a broad stretch.

I moved. With the suddenness of a leaping fish, I hurled myself from the water. The horse, terrified, reared high. It was not enough to unseat Golahka, expert horseman that he was, but it did unbalance him. He rocked backwards, and before he could regain control I seized my chance. With all my strength I pushed at his hip. Taken by surprise by my audacity, this was enough to topple him. He fell in the dust on one side of the mare, and I sprang onto her back from the other, urging the animal homewards before he could respond.

Thus I returned to our settlement of painted tepees after my first trial: weaponless, without supplies, dripping and sodden.

On horseback.

Triumphant.

I had done as Golahka commanded, no more, yet still I feared his temper as I waited for his return.

I should not have done so. He walked into our camp soon after my hasty arrival, seemingly afflicted with a heavy limp. The eyes of our people were upon him. Chodini himself came to meet him, to ask how he had fared amongst the Chokenne. Golahka gave swift reply to the question that buzzed in all minds like the hornet.

"They will come," he said, his voice carrying so that all our tribe could hear. "Our brothers ride the warpath with us!"

Many nodded, satisfied at such an outcome. A surge of battle lust passed through the warriors. The very air seemed to taste of it.

The women, who had paused while Golahka spoke, now went back to the tasks they had been engaged in. I waited, uncertain what I should do. Golahka relished my awkwardness. He rubbed his hip elaborately, as if it gave him much pain. I knew it could not; any warrior that truly suffered would give no sign of it. This was but play to heighten my discomfort.

When Chodini asked what ailed him, Golahka replied without expression, "I was ambushed."

Chodini was surprised. "Ambushed? By whom?" he asked.

Golahka looked at me. His eyes burned into my face while I tried, and failed, to hold his stare. "It was a water snake," he said at last. "A treacherous serpent. It took me quite unawares."

I felt, rather than saw, the eyes of Chodini upon me as he tried to understand Golahka's meaning. And then the sombre face of Golahka broke into a smile, and his ringing laugh sounded throughout the camp.

"Siki bested me," he told our chief quietly, as if he disbelieved the content of his own words.

"You were bested by a novice?" asked Chodini. "You?"

"Indeed! A mere stripling! But this novice has cunning, my chief. Be glad she rides with us. I would not choose her as my enemy."

Golahka turned to me then and said, "You discovered much upon the mountain, Siki; do not rest easy, even when your journey's end is in sight. It was a lesson well learnt." He laughed once more, and then added, "Ay, it was a lesson well taught too." With that he left me to walk with Chodini and give him news of Goyenne, his beloved daughter; and the great chief Sotchez.

Thus dismissed, I led the mare to where the horses grazed, smiling to myself. But as I walked, my arms began to prickle and bump as though a sudden chill cooled the air. It was as if I had entered a crevasse of deep shadow where the sun could not send forth its rays. I looked to see from whence the cold had come.

Keste.

He stood near the tepee of Dahtet, dripping icy scorn as I dripped water from the river. He said nothing, but I felt his eyes, unblinking, upon me, as though he sought to peel off my flesh; expose raw muscle; see what weakness lay hidden beneath my skin.

His words, when they came, stopped my breath. "You think you will be a warrior?" he said softly. "You will not. You have your coward father's blood. Some day it will out, and all will see you for what you are."

He turned and stalked away between the tepees before I had drawn sufficient air to demand his meaning.

With trembling hands, I smoothed the mare, checking she had suffered no ills from her journey that might need tending. Then I released her to the herd. As I watched her scrape the ground and roll, kicking her legs wildly in the air, I fretted over Keste's words. But then I was stirred with fresh resolve.

I would not fear Keste, nor quake before the malice of one who was not yet a warrior. I – who had bested Golahka in a trial of wits; who had vowed to find Tazhi's slayer and kill him – would neither fear nor fight one of my own tribe. I would treat no Black Mountain Apache as my enemy; thus was my solemn, silent vow made before Ussen.

What sadness, then, that Keste did not do the same.

Golahka rested but one night before he moved again, departing at sunrise on a fresh horse to seek the Dendhi Apache, as he had sought the Chokenne, to ask for their help. This time, I knew he would permit no follower. He had to go forth alone.

Golahka's wife, Tehineh, had been of the Dendhi, and had moved to the Black Mountain Apache when she wed Golahka. He had to carry the word of her death to her kinsfolk. Terrible would be the anguish he unloosed. Tehineh's aged father yet lived. It was known amongst my people that the old man had been loath to part with his youngest daughter. Perhaps he had disliked the youthful arrogance of Golahka, for he had then been but seventeen summers old, newly admitted to the Hilaneh council of warriors, and young to be thus honoured. Perhaps her father wished to keep her with him to guard against the loneliness of his coming age. Perhaps he simply loved Tehineh too much to endure such a parting, for Tehineh was beloved by all who looked on her.

The love that burned between Golahka and Tehineh had been plain for all to see, and yet still her father had resisted the match, demanding not one or two good horses as marriage settlement as would most fathers. No ... Tehineh's father had demanded ten of horse, and ten of beef – seemingly an impossible price to lay upon his daughter's head. Golahka had said nothing, but departed at once, and returned some days later, driving a vast herd before him. Still he did not speak, but sat upon his horse and extended his hand to Tehineh.

She had never returned to her tribe.

Golahka would not stay with the Dendhi and daily endure the enmity of her father, but neither had he wished to return to the Hilaneh, for they were of a peaceful disposition, much given to the growing of corn and melons. Golahka was no farmer. Instead he had joined with Chodini, for the great chief's wisdom and prowess as a warrior were renowned throughout the Apache nation. Golahka had come with Tehineh and his widowed mother, Nahasgah, and become one of the Black Mountain Apache.

Fierce now would be the grief of Tehineh's father. Raw indeed would be his pain. Deep would burn his hatred of Golahka. Such private things were not to be looked upon by strangers. I stayed in our settlement and brooded.

I could not understand Keste's words, and yet neither could I dismiss them. Jealous spite had made him goad me, and yet I felt some measure of truth lay hidden in what he said. A secret lurked darkly in the shadows. I desired to know it – to drag it into the light.

At sunrise, I did not join the men in the hunt, nor the women in their endless gathering of nuts and berries. Instead I went to the horses.

I chose the dark mare – I had a fondness for this animal – and took a hunting club I had newly fashioned. I rode alone, intent on killing rabbits. I could not fail to see Keste's mocking smile as I turned from the company of men and boys. I did not doubt that he thought of our last hunt, and believed his words had stung me. He thought I was beaten by him; I let him think so. Chee extended a hand as if he would draw me to the hunters, but I turned from him also, for I craved solitude.

I hunted hard that day, and far, galloping across the upland meadows after skittish rabbits. The mare was but newly taken from the Mexicans, and had not yet become accustomed to Apache ways. At the start of our riding she was alarmed when, grasping her mane in one hand, I slid down her side and swung my club near her galloping hooves. I missed my first kill, for the mare jumped sideways in panic and sent me rolling upon the grass. But when she felt her freedom she did not run back to the camp to join the other horses, but rather stood, eyeing me warily. Curiosity kept her there, and I liked her the more for it.

I approached her quietly, speaking soothing nonsense. There is a place on the neck where a horse cannot scratch itself; and so, in a herd, animals will often stand shoulder to shoulder – one facing the other's tail – that they may bite and rub each other's necks. I found the place and scratched the mare until her lip drooped and she began to nuzzle my shoulder in return. We stood thus for some time, and when I felt her trust settle upon me I did what I should have done at first – I let her see and smell the club. I rolled it over her skin and down her legs, passing it between her hooves so that she lost her fear of the weapon.

Springing upon the mare's back, I rode once more. She was swift to learn: an eager, intelligent mount. As a rabbit broke cover, she pricked her ears, and at my bidding ran in pursuit of the animal. I laughed aloud at her willingness, joying in her vibrant spirit as we galloped. I made my first kill when the sun was high in the wide sky.

When the sun at last began to dip below the horizon, I turned homewards, ten or more rabbits slung across the mare's neck.

The flesh of a rabbit is not as highly prized as the flesh of the deer, but Dahtet's family were glad of my offering. The deer hunt had returned with but two feeble animals, and I took grim pleasure from the galled look that flashed across Keste's face when I rode into our camp.

"Rabbits!" I heard him mutter scornfully. "The prey of infants!"

I said nothing, for in truth, when the camp is settled in one place as we now were, warriors do not often waste themselves in hunting such small game. I wondered what Golahka would have said of my lonely pursuit. But Chee leapt to my defence.

"Maybe so," he told Keste calmly. "But a rabbit will fill an empty belly as well as any deer."

Keste spat upon the ground. I did not smile at Chee – to do so would only inflame Keste further. But my eyes spoke words of thanks.

Having given my kill to Dahtet and her mother, I set about helping them skin the creatures, but Dahtet took the knife from my hands.

"You are to be a warrior, Siki," she said. "You must let me do this work. Besides, you will nick the skins and spoil them."

She spoke truth. Many times Nahasgah had despaired at my ineptitude in preparing hides. It was this that made Dahtet bid me cease, not my status as a novice warrior, for warriors must know and understand all the tasks of the tribe lest they should ever need them: they must stitch and sew and cook as well as any woman, as indeed the women of our tribe must shoot a bow and use a knife as deftly as a man.

The quick, nimble fingers of Dahtet skinned the rabbits in the light of the fire. The shadows of the flickering flames seemed to set the painted animals on the tepee walls dancing. I sat watching the little red and black creatures leap and spin. For a slow, indrawn breath my sight blurred, and the beasts seemed to gather together and take the shape of a child – a strange, pale infant – but even as I looked the image dissolved and vanished and the animals were painted icons once more.

Dahtet talked with her mother as she worked, a soft stream of words that meant little but were a healing balm to my troubled spirits. Wrapped in their familiar warmth, I slept.

Golahka returned from the Dendhi with welcome news. Willingly they had agreed to ride the warpath with us. Once winter had passed, three Apache tribes would meet, and the warriors would set forth to spill Mexican blood.

I was glad of it, and yet felt piercing sadness to see that all warmth, all humour, had been driven from Golahka's face by his time amongst the Dendhi. The rawness of their mourning had torn all but hardness from him. When he returned to our Black Mountain settlement, his eyes were the eyes of a dead man once more. He looked as though he would never smile again, never laugh amongst his kinsmen, never mock my attempts at ambush. Sorely I raged with fresh anger; it seemed the Mexicans who had slain our loved ones had also done mortal injury to the spirit of a great warrior. Black burned my hatred of our enemy when Golahka gathered those who would become warriors around his fire to begin our training.

I had proved my worthiness when I met Golahka's challenge, and thus I sat, chin high, awaiting his instruction. Through the long winter that lay ahead, he would teach us mastery of our weapons and of ourselves. When spring came, if we had performed well the arduous tasks demanded of us, we might be permitted to accompany the men on the warpath as their servants. To become a warrior, a novice must make four such journeys. Only then will he be admitted to the warrior council.

Chee was beside me. He too was only now taking his first step along this path; we began as equals. Opposite sat Keste. He had followed the warriors three times before, and thought himself already a man. He was within one journey of achieving the status he longed for. And yet his eyes gleamed with resentment as he glared at his companions. It was as though Keste thought that renown came only in a limited supply, and that another novice in doing well would consume and diminish the portion of fame he believed was owed to him. I knew Keste brimmed with rancour that I was amongst the youths Golahka would teach.

There were others too: Ishta, who was perhaps sixteen summers, and had followed the warpath twice before. Naite, the son of Chodini's brother, a tall youth of similar age to Keste. Like Keste he had completed three journeys, but Naite's ambition did not mar his judgement. Last to join us was Huten, who was one summer younger than myself and Chee.

I was surprised indeed that Huten had chosen to join us. He was hard and fit, as are all Apache children; boy and girl alike are strong and fleet of foot, and all must know the rules of survival. But Huten possessed a mild, sweet temper, and had little of the warrior about him. When he had been sent into the mountains alone to prove his worthiness, he had never entirely disappeared from view. For seven sunrises he had lingered on the mountain, just within sight of his mother's tepee. He kept his silence and spoke to no one, but he had had no relish for the task. I was astonished that he persisted thus with training. Not all boys will become warriors, and amongst our people no shame falls on those who do not wish to walk the warrior's path. In our play as children, I had always thought Huten would be one of those who walked proudly amongst the women on his own, distinct trail, as I now walked mine amongst the men. But the Mexicans had also done mortal injury to his sweet spirit, for his grandmother lay amongst the slain at Koskineh, and his eyes now shone bright with anguish.

"Pain," said Golahka. "Pain and its mastery are what I teach today. Hear me, for I tell you now that pain can be overcome. No matter how deep it bites, it can be conquered. To face suffering with no fear: this is the way of the Apache warrior."

He held out his arm and placed a withered leaf of sage upon it. Then, taking a flaming stick from the fire, he lit the leaf. It caught at once, the flame flaring high and bright, and we watched as it burned and at last crumbled into flaked ashes. The smell of scorched flesh and hair was strong, and the arm of Golahka was marked with a searing blister where the leaf had been. But he made no sound. Not a cry, not a whisper. No muscle had twitched, and his eyes had not narrowed with pain. It was as if the arm was not his, so little did it trouble him.

And now Golahka bade us extend our own arms towards the flames. Around the circle he walked, running a scorched stick that glowed red from where it had lain in the fire down the length of our arms. Try as we might, one by one we recoiled, drawing our arms back with a sudden breath of shock. It was instinct to do so: none would willingly endure fire. And yet this was what Golahka wished us to do.

"Feel it," he murmured. "Know it. Find its limits. Go beyond it." Thus saying, he placed a leaf upon the arm of Keste, and lit it.

At once, Keste's neck became rigid, the sinews standing proud of his skin as the roots of the oak upon the earth, his jaw clenched with the fierceness of his determination not to cry out. Sweat beaded at his hairline and gathered upon his lip. But he made no sound, and as the leaf crumbled into ashes, he earned words of praise from Golahka. Only I knew how much Keste's effort had cost him. I sat facing him, and I had seen his pupils widen with the horror of intense pain. I knew Keste would not forgive me for seeing the weakness that lay beneath his skin. When he fixed his eyes upon me, they were dark with loathing.

Huten faced his trial next, and did not endure long. The leaf had scarce begun to burn before he snatched at his wrist with his other hand to stop himself shaking the leaf free. Even so, long before it had crumbled into ash, Huten had thrown off the burning sage with a cry. He sat, tears streaming down his face, whether of the hurt to his arm or of the distress at his failure I could not tell. I was not sure that Huten knew which caused him to suffer more. Golahka said nothing to worsen his ordeal, but moved on to Ishta and Naite, while

Huten struggled to compose himself.

Both endured the leaf for little longer than Huten, their bodies at last instinctively throwing off that which burned them. Chee too struggled hard to maintain his silence. He did better than both Ishta and Naite, keeping the leaf on his arm until it turned to ash, but his face and body contorted with the effort, and his lips bled where he bit them.

And then Golahka came to me.

I held my arm towards him and he placed the dry leaf upon my skin. So intent was I, so determined that I must succeed in this trial, that my arm seemed to grow large and heavy and become burdensome. The nerves prickled at the leaf's rough dryness. Next I felt the burning heat of the flaming stick he bore towards me. He lit the leaf and my body surged in response, wanting to quench the flame that licked and curled around the leaf. I resisted it, tensing even as I had seen Keste do. The pain rose and rose and threatened to engulf me. My back was hard and rigid. As I stiffened in an effort to rise above and away from the pain, suddenly I knew I could not thus evade it. The only way to endure was to pass beyond it, to a different way of being. And in an instant I knew I had been in that place once before – when I had sat that long, dead time in the pine tree at Koskineh, swaying in the wind, my head pressed hard against the rough bark. There I had found a place where I felt nothing.

It was as though I plunged into a mountain pool. I stopped resisting. With a deep, calming breath, I dived into the pain. I found its heart and I swam through it. And came to a place far beyond, where my body ceased to matter.

My mind did not return when the leaf had burnt to ashes. I know not how long I stayed thus. It was only when Golahka took my hand and called me four times by my name that my still-open eyes at last saw the world about me. The sun had moved; it seemed to me as if it had suddenly leapt across the sky. Keste, Huten, Chee, Ishta and Naite were there no longer. Golahka alone beheld me, his black eyes gleaming with something other than grief. Something that could have been excitement.

"Siki," he said quietly, "do you have Power?"

Power. Power to see the future. Power to feel the spirits of the earth; to taste their magic and know their minds. And – for some – Power to hear the voice of Ussen, the Life Giver.

My father had not possessed it, and neither had my mother, but amongst many of the Apache Power flows freely; it does not belong only to the medicine man. The gift – if it comes – comes with adulthood. A boy may feel it when he embarks upon his training as a warrior. A girl will know Power during the four-day ritual of her womanhood ceremony. I had had no ceremony, for lacking relatives there had been no one to make my feast, and thus when I left childhood I had not heard the voice of Ussen.

Many of our tribe possess Power in some measure: a mother may sense when her child is in danger; a wife may know of her husband's death in battle before word is brought of it. But there are fewer to whom Ussen will whisper. Golahka was amongst those favoured ones, and was thus greatly revered as a shaman of war.

But I had heard no voice, seen no vision, and I told Golahka this. I had conquered my pain. That was all. So I believed. But Golahka made a noise in his throat: a thoughtful, considering grunt as though the matter was not yet finished. He questioned me no further, for Power is a sacred, private thing, not to be spoken of lightly. And yet I felt sure that Golahka did not dismiss my trance as swiftly as I had done.

He bade me go, instructing me to partake of the food that Dahtet and her mother had prepared, for the sun was now low in the sky, but I did not return to the tepee at once. Rather I took myself to the river, where I might be alone.

It was not until I sat watching the dark water flow over the stones that I remembered the face of my father. I had seen him at Koskineh, when my mind had been so crazed with horror at the slaughter below me that it had conjured his image from my memory. Thus I had thought. And I had considered that the glimpse of his terror-widened eyes, and even my dream of him running, were fevered imaginings sprung from the wretchedness of grief. But was it possible that the visions came from elsewhere? Had Ussen placed them before me?

My heart pounded with excitement even as my mind puzzled over what I had seen. My father anguished. Exhausted. And – somehow spreading from him as though he were its source – the stain creeping like a shadow across the broad plain.

If it was indeed Ussen who had drawn these images in my mind... For what purpose?

Golahka continued our training. He was our teacher, our guide, our shaman, but often it seemed he was our tormentor also.

Daily he made us run before dawn, pounding the trail to the mountain top carrying water in our mouths. This we could not swallow, but had to spit out at his feet on our return to learn how to govern our breathing. When the days grew cold, and the air sharp, Golahka made us plunge into the ice-encrusted river. Only briefly could we warm ourselves at the fire, before we must plunge into the freezing water once more, without murmur, without complaint.

It became easier for me to find the place where I felt nothing, and to hold myself there until pain and discomfort had passed. But Huten was not so fortunate. He was determined to edge along the warrior's path, but for him the trail was precipitous, and at each faltering step it appeared he might fall headlong into an abyss. Each test, each trial of agility or endurance, was cruel agony. He did not harden and flourish as the rest of us did; every day sapped him more, and it seemed sometimes that sweet-tempered, mild Huten would melt away with the ice when the sun came.

One morning, Golahka led his pupils down from the mountains onto the plain. Each of us carried a slingshot. We were set to fight.

It was a familiar game amongst the boys to flick stones at each other: to dodge, to aim, to strike one's opponent. When groups of youths from our brother tribes met, they would sometimes hold pitched battles amongst themselves. I had often watched such contests, but as a girl, I had never been part of one. The sling was an unfamiliar weapon to me.

Chee knew my lack of prowess with the weapon; and so, as we took our places for the fight, he stood facing me, intending that he should be my opponent. Chee would not drive me hard. Chee would not aim to injure me.

Perhaps Golahka intended that I should be pushed to my limits, or perhaps he meant to preserve Huten's brittle pride, for when he saw where Chee had placed himself, Golahka shook his head, and indicated that someone else should take his place. Chee he paired with Huten. Facing me stood Keste.

Golahka, I knew, had seen the enmity Keste bore me. Keste did not trouble to conceal either his jealousy or his contempt. Indeed, before Golahka had given the command to begin, Keste had picked up a stone the size of my eye and slung his first shot. I dodged, but it struck a stinging blow sharp against my elbow, breaking the skin, and making me cry out.

I looked at Golahka, but before words of girlish protest could fall from my mouth, the great warrior spoke.

"On this day, you have no friends. On this day, you fight. There is no mercy. No softness.

You think the Mexicans will be fair? You think the Mexicans will wait until you are ready? You think the Mexicans will show compassion for your weakness?"

Golahka did not look at me, but I felt the rebuke in his words.

"The one you face now is your enemy," he continued, and as I glanced at Keste I knew he spoke perfect truth.

Upon Golahka's command we began.

To me, it seemed suddenly as if the sky rained stones. Keste had quietly filled his hands with them while Golahka spoke, or maybe he had picked them up as we walked. He did not trouble with the slingshot in his first assault but simply hurled two handfuls of flint at my face. I could not dodge so many, but turned away that they might not strike my eyes, and felt many stinging blows against my head and shoulders. But already I searched for a stone of my own, and fixed it into my slingshot. As I spun back to face him, I flicked it low – at his shins, where he would not expect it – and was rewarded with a crack as it hit bone.

Thereafter, Keste made a strange opponent. His desire to hurt me flared so strong it made him clumsy. He used such savage force to propel his stones, it was easy to see where he aimed and to step aside lightly and let them thud into the dirt. But I had no mastery of the weapon. My one shot at his shins was a lucky one, and I found I could not load the sling while I dodged his assault. He was so certain of his superiority, so certain of his skill. A simple task, then, to deceive him.

As Keste fired a stone at my face, I turned slowly, and let it strike my raised arm. Blood flowed and I stumbled in the dust, falling awkwardly to my knees.

Despite Golahka's words, all knew that this was a contest amongst members of the same tribe, not a fight between enemies. We might cause injury, but it was not the intention to kill. I was downed, and thus it should have been time to cease our fight. Had Keste done so then, he would have been declared the victor.

But I had judged him right: Keste could not let me rest where I had fallen. He ran swiftly across the plain, a rock the size of my head clutched in his hands. I kept my chin down, seemingly hurt, seemingly beaten. When he stopped and stood triumphant over me, he called my name that I might raise my eyes and look at him. He wished me to see his victory.

"Do you cower?" he sneered. "How like your father you are."

He raised the stone high above his head, that he might bring it down and crush my face.

It was not so. As I began to lift my gaze to his, my hand closed upon the flint I held, and I flicked it sharp and hard between his eyes. My aim was good. He recoiled, dropping his rock, clutching his nose. When his hand came away, it was bloodied. In fury, he dived at me.

It was then the voice of Golahka whipped across the plain. "Enough!" It was a voice none dared disobey. At a sign from Golahka, Keste – shaking with anger – followed as the great warrior led us back towards the mountains and our camp.

Chee waited as I rose from the dust. His face too was bloodied, as though Huten had struck him many times. I did not doubt that Chee had chosen not to hear Golahka's words; he had been merciful with Huten, at the cost of his own blood, and I was glad of it.

We walked together, side by side.

"Dahtet will be much displeased," Chee said, laughing. "You have spoilt the pretty nose of Keste."

I laughed too, but my heart contracted at his words. All were aware, then, of Dahtet's liking for Keste. It did not take the voice of Ussen, whispering in my ear, to know that nothing good would come of it.

We walked in silence awhile, and then I said, "Keste spoke of my father…"

"To what purpose?"

"He called him coward."

Chee frowned and shook his head. His eyes showed nothing but puzzlement, and I saw that whatever secret knowledge Keste seemed to have, it had not reached the ears of Chee. And yet I could not leave the matter to rest.

"The raid from which he did not return…" I began. "Was not Keste's father of that party?"

"Punte? Indeed. But so was my own. Golahka too. And they have never said aught."

"But perhaps Punte saw something that … displeased him. He may have spoken of it to Keste."

At this Chee laughed. "It is not so! Keste's words have no substance, Siki! He plucks them from the air to torment you. You must not let him!"

I said no more, and for some time we walked in easy silence. But then Chee spoke.

"Golahka has questioned me of the hunt," he said quietly.

I stopped then, and looked at his face that I might understand his meaning.

Chee shrugged. "I saw nothing, Siki. I was reaching for an arrow when the herd scattered, and then I saw you run." He laughed with pleasure. "Such a run! I told Golahka of your swiftness. All stood amazed by your feat."

This was but little comfort. My stomach stirred with uneasiness that Golahka had thus spoken to Chee. I had dismissed Keste's false reports as pettish jealousy. I had kept my silence, and not confronted him with his untruths. Now I wondered if I had been wise to do so. Amongst our people the word of a warrior is binding. His honesty – his veracity – must be beyond question. It seemed this small squabble had grown into a larger creature which might threaten my reputation and devour my honour. For if Golahka believed the word of Keste, he must doubt mine. And twice – in taking his horse, and now in tricking Keste – I had shown Golahka my capacity for deceit.

I wondered if, in pairing me with Keste, Golahka had not been setting us both a challenge. A challenge which one of us would fail.

Thereafter, Golahka kept a distance between myself and Keste. In each trial, Keste excelled. He was fierce and strong; his skill in tracking was unsurpassed. With a bow his aim never faltered – each arrow struck its target exactly as he intended. Desire for fame and prestige drove him on to greater and greater prowess. Keste, it seemed, wished to shine as bright as the sun, so that while he walked the living earth all eyes would be dazzled by his glory, and none should notice the smaller stars that also hung in the heavens. It was easy to see that he would make a bold, courageous warrior. And yet ... I felt something brittle was there too. Something that might yet shatter.

As the days lengthened, and the trees' tight buds burst open, our people at last prepared to break camp. There was a freshness in the air; the tang of sweet, new growth; a savour of excitement; the very wind seemed to breathe the promise of revenge. The mood of the warriors was as tense and heavy as the heated air before a thunderstorm.

In the moon of fresh leaves, we were to meet with our brother tribes in the Chokenne mountains. There we would make camp, leaving our women and children safe in a hidden, secret place, while the warriors followed the warpath into Mexico.

All were busy with the tasks of removal. Tepees were dismantled, and the long poles fashioned into litters that would be dragged behind our horses. These were stacked with hides, rolled and bundled tightly; baskets filled with provisions; and water jugs for our journey. Our camp was all confusion as it became smaller and smaller and finally shrank to nothing. The trodden grass and the burnt dark rings of our fires showed we had been here, but swiftly would these be hidden by new shoots of spring grass. Within the waxing and waning of a single moon no trace of our winter camp would remain upon the earth.

At dawn we set forth, following the same way we had passed twelve moons before, when Tazhi and I had travelled with such joy, such lightness of spirit. A different mood it was that now possessed the tribe: we moved with the dark impatience of those hungry for battle. And now I was no longer the girl who failed always to achieve mastery of the women's craft. I carried Tazhi's spear, the flint blade gleaming – black as the eyes of Golahka – with its thirst for justice.

And yet I knew not how to find the man who had slain Tazhi. If I were to accompany the warriors, it would be as a novice. I would not be amongst those who fought on the battlefield. But even as I prayed to Ussen that he grant me my revenge, Tazhi's spear seemed to hum with energy in my hand as if it were a living thing. And with each step I took, I felt a growing certainty that I would face Tazhi's slayer.

And I would kill him.

In a few days, we were deep in the Chokenne range, and there it was that the Black Mountain, the Dendhi and the Chokenne Apache gathered. The place was well chosen – a hidden plateau high in the mountains watered by a gushing stream. The faces of rock that bound the camp ensured that it was easily protected from an advancing enemy. A single winding path was the only route by which a horse could pass, and along this trail many boulders and stones were placed that could be thrown down if an enemy rode upon it. In the warriors' absence, the Mexicans could not steal upon the camp without being seen. If, by chance, they came in overwhelming numbers, the women and children would have much time to flee.

Here it was that the tribes came together. Never had I seen so many of my people together in one place, nor so many tepees facing the rising sun, nor heard so many voices lift together to welcome the morning. In the warmth of the quickening spring, while the women chattered and sang, and the children played, the warriors of all three tribes met in council. Golahka, the great warrior, was first to speak.

"My brothers, we have come together for a solemn purpose: to avenge our loved ones, blood for blood. The Mexicans shall rue their treachery. They shall grieve, and they shall mourn; they shall suffer, even as we have done. I know the land. I will lead you to their city. By hidden ways we shall approach their homes. Let them have no warning of our intent. As they came upon us – secretly and in silence – so will we come upon them."

All were agreed to travel on foot into Mexico. On foot, the warriors would not be seen. The Mexicans should not know of our approach until we were upon them. It was a plan of sense, but for long, thudding heartbeats I cursed it. Golahka, I thought, had promised that I would be with the war party. But much of the novice's task is to care for the horses, and if the warriors journeyed on foot I dreaded they would have no need of me. I struggled to keep my silence; I would not help myself by calling out or begging that I might come. Biting my lip, I stared at the dust while the council drew to an end.

As the warriors dispersed to their families to make ready for what lay ahead, Golahka came to the youths he had trained all the long winter. Chodini was with him, and it was he who spoke, first to Keste.

"I wish that you remain here," Chodini said.

I heard Keste's sharply indrawn breath and felt the strength of his shock – for indeed I was as surprised as he by Chodini's words – but neither Chodini nor Golahka responded. Chodini was our chief, and yet he could not order Keste to remain. But only a simpleton would go against the expressed wish of one so wise and well beloved as our chief, and Keste was no simpleton.

"Our people must be guarded," Chodini continued. "Some warriors must remain. In this task I trust you as a man, and not a novice."

It was an honour for Chodini to speak to him so, and a very great honour to be trusted with the care and protection of the tribe. Despite this, Keste's eyes spilt gall. If Keste joined the warpath, it would be his fourth such journey. When he returned, he might be admitted to the council as a full warrior. Thereafter he would be free to marry. No wonder, then, that he protested with such vigour.

"I wish to come." He spoke so loudly that the birds in the trees near by took flight.

"Our people must be protected." Chodini's words came softly, yet none could doubt the threat contained within them.

Keste faltered only briefly. "I will come," he said hotly.

And then Golahka stepped forward and spoke, his voice little more than a whisper. "Keste," he said, "tell me this. When you hunted the deer, did Siki truly scatter the herd? Or were they poised for flight before she moved?"

Cold horror clutched my stomach to hear Golahka speak so. To talk of this now, at such a time, in such a place! I knew not what it meant.

It seemed I balanced on the edge of an abyss while I waited for Keste's answer.

Yet Keste too was alarmed by Golahka's question. He opened his mouth to speak, then closed it. Opened it once more, but made no sound.

And then I knew why Keste could say nothing in reply. If he spoke truth now, he must confess he had lied before. If he maintained his false report, Golahka would call upon others who had hunted. For I thought I saw in the warrior's blackly glinting eyes that someone – I knew not who – had seen the herd startle before I ran and had told him of it.

Keste also saw what lay in Golahka's expression. His jaw clenched tightly shut, he turned and walked silently away. Keste was defeated, but in defeat he was as full of menace as the trapped and wounded bear.

I could not help but ask, "Who saw the deer startle?" I wished to know the name of the hunter who had spoken in defence of me.

Golahka's eyes showed nothing when he answered, "No one."

I frowned in confusion, but before I could ask more questions, Golahka said softly, "It was my own judgement told me who spoke true. None but Keste saw what you did. He has condemned himself."

I saw the look that passed between Golahka and our chief and I began to understand why Keste had been detained thus. They mistrusted his temper. They mistrusted his desire for fame that burned too bright, obscuring his judgement and causing him to burst with hot jealousy against any who might overshadow him. Keste, I saw in their looks, could not be relied upon; and on the warpath the warriors needed those at their backs who could be trusted without question.

Into the silence that followed, Chodini spoke once more. To Ishta he explained, "This is a hazardous journey. Many will be the hardships; great will be the danger. I cannot make a promise to your parents that I will keep you safe. Let them decide if you follow the warpath, or if you remain to protect the camp." To Naite he said, "You are my brother's son: let him choose what you are to do."

Ishta and Naite departed to talk with their loved ones.

Huten did not wait to hear Chodini speak. "I must stay amongst the women," he said, his voice tight as the drawn bowstring. "You need not tell me so." Tears began to brim upon his lids, and he turned swiftly and fled before he could shame himself before his chief.

There was a short silence; then Chodini turned to Chee. My friend hung his head, waiting calmly to do as he was requested. But here Golahka intervened.

"This boy has the qualities to make a fine warrior. If he wishes to come – if his parents permit it – we would have need of him."

Chee's chin lifted proudly. Golahka honoured him speaking thus; no parent would refuse him. Chee's return to Mexico was certain. He nodded gladly, and then ran to spread word amongst his family.

Golahka's black eyes then settled upon me. I stood, feeling the weight of them, but not daring to look into his face.

"Full well I know this novice wishes to join us," he said.

I scarcely breathed.

Chodini seemed troubled. "She is but slight for such a task."

"Indeed, my chief," conceded Golahka. "Yet she was wronged at Koskineh. She has sworn vengeance."

There was a pause, while Chodini weighed the warrior's words. Golahka spoke again. "My chief, truly I think she must come."

"Must?"

"Indeed. For if we tell her nay, she will but follow on her own, and who knows then what ill may befall her. Is it not so, Siki?"

It was then I dared look up, and saw the face of Golahka creased with teasing mirth. And the loved, wise head of our chief nodding his assent.

I was to go. I should not have doubted it. Ishta and Naite were likewise to follow the warpath. This was not the first time they had accompanied the warriors; they were already familiar with the tasks they must perform. But Chee and I had much to learn before the morning, and Golahka spent a long time that day instructing us in the duties we would undertake while with the war party. Sitting on the soft dry earth in the shade of a tall pine, we breathed in Golahka's lessons even as we inhaled the scent of the tree's new growth.

War was a solemn, spiritual matter, Golahka told us, and we must learn the sacred words in the war language of the Apache. The common names of things were not to be used: our knives were called instead "that with which we cut"; our hearts became "that by which we live"; and the sacred pollen with which we would daub our faces "that which makes life". In this way was the war party's purpose sanctified, for battle is not a daily occurrence, and must not be undertaken lightly. Many were the rites we should observe and the rituals we should follow – and all had to be done correctly, lest we offend the spirits and call down misfortune upon our heads.

"You are also to perform the heavy work of the camp: collect wood, light fires, carry water, cook, and keep watch while the warriors take their rest. You must be first to rise, and last to sleep. You are not to speak unless invited to do so, and must then give but short replies. You will eat only such food as you are offered once others have taken their fill. This you must eat cold…"

In short, we were to serve, and to endure all hardships silently. In doing so we but followed the example of our chief, Chodini; as we would serve the warriors, so he served his people. To become a warrior, first must one learn to observe and supply the needs of others. This is the way of the Apache.

Such lightness of childish spirit as had survived deep within me was now extinguished by the solemnity of the task that lay ahead. Henceforth I could only wait for our departure, which would come on the morrow, and while I did so, the sacred duties I would have to observe lay heavy upon my shoulders.

*   *   *

When Golahka had finished his oration, I returned to Dahtet's family, brooding upon what was to come. At first I thought the tepee empty, but then from within I heard the soft sound of weeping. Lifting the flap, I entered, and found Dahtet.

It seemed that stalking from the warriors' council, Keste had unleashed his temper upon her. As she went to collect water, she had approached him and asked gently, as was her way, what angered him. He had not raised a hand to her, but his words had cut her as deeply as would his flint-bladed knife. I questioned her, but she told me nothing of what he had said. Instead, she began to speak of Toah, the Dendhi chief, and his wife, Kaywin, sister to Golahka.

"They say Toah was cruel to her... That when he was but a boy, he visited the Hilaneh tribe of Kaywin often with his parents. He knew not how to speak to her; instead he lay in wait, and when she passed by he stole her berries and scattered her mesquite nuts upon the ground. It was his shyness, you see, that made him cruel. Yet when they were both grown, she willingly became his wife. And now, you see, he is a good husband."

I knew why Dahtet spoke thus. But Keste was not Toah.

Toah was cursed with a misshapen mouth that sometimes made his speech difficult to understand.

As a boy, it had been torment to him. Even now, in councils, often his leading warrior would speak the words aloud that Toah whispered haltingly in his ear. Yet Toah was full of wisdom, a fierce and warlike leader who served his tribe well and was much loved by his people.

It was not youthful awkwardness, not the shyness of a troubled boy, that drove Keste's cruelty. Keste would not be softened by marriage. I felt compelled to speak my thoughts.

"Dahtet..." I spoke clumsily. "Keste burns with ambition. It makes him act without mercy. His temper..."

I could not continue, for Dahtet was shaking her head.

"You are wrong, Siki," she said. "He will make a famed warrior. His ambition runs high, it is true, but so it does with all young men."

"No ... it is more than that. He does not wish to remain here while others follow the warpath. It has made him dangerous."

Although Keste had shown his cruelty to her, still Dahtet leapt to his defence. It was as if she stood in the middle of a swirling torrent, Keste the rock upon which she had chosen to stand. If she once saw the truth of him, she would be lost, swept away – gone.

"He is disappointed," she said, "but this will pass. He is a good man, and a fine one. If he wishes me to become his wife I will do so gladly."

I spoke slowly, attempting to pick my words as carefully as I selected stones with which to fashion arrowheads. "I do not believe Keste will make a kind – a loving – husband."

Dahtet's fury loosed itself upon me. "You believe you know him; you do not." Her voice rose higher as she spoke, and became hard and brittle. "You see only his anger, because it is you who angers him. He says you are unnatural. Strange. An offence against the laws of Ussen. He does not think our chief should permit you to follow this path you have chosen. And perhaps you should not."

Had I possessed sufficient sense, I would have walked far from Dahtet when she attacked me thus. It was plain she would not heed the words of a girl who had turned from marriage and motherhood before they had even been offered. What did I know of such womanly concerns? What right had I to speak to her of them?

And yet, stupidly, I felt I must persist. "Keste is not trusted by our chief, Dahtet. It is not I alone who dislikes him. Golahka—"

At the mention of the warrior's name, Dahtet's face became a sneering mask, grotesquely distorted as though she had been slashed with a knife – shocking in one as gentle as she.

"Ah, yes ... Golahka," she spat with contempt. "Does he not always leap to your defence? Keste says you have bewitched him."

Horror swept through me. To be spoken of as a witch – one who has Power and uses it for ill against others – was a terrible thing. If such a rumour took hold amongst our tribe it would imperil my life, for a proven witch is not allowed to live. I knew Keste would not speak this way openly while Chodini gave me his protection. But still I was dismayed that he had even spoken the words aloud to Dahtet – that his mind had begun to run thus – and that Dahtet had seemingly started to believe him.

I did not wish to hear more. "Enough," I said quietly, turning from her with a heavy heart. We spoke no more.

Taking my weapons, I went from the tepee.

And so I left Dahtet to her fate, as she left me to mine.

What remained of the day passed slowly. Many times I packed and removed and packed once more the stone-headed arrows in my quiver. Most warriors, I observed, carried arrows tipped with points of metal, and the heads of their lances were fashioned from the blades of Mexican swords. I preferred stone, for stone is a living thing and sings with its own life even as the wood of my bow and the sinew of its string.

The crescent moon was beginning to rise. I smoothed the head of Tazhi's spear until it shone in the light. It would have its fill of blood before the moon waxed full. As the sun at last sank behind the mountains, a dark shadow swept across the plateau where we camped, bringing with it a sudden chill, and bringing to mind the dream I had once had of my father.

Amongst the gathered tribes, there were men and women who had known him, although I could ask none for their knowledge. There is much power in a name. Even the living must use each other's names with care. We do not speak of the dead, lest the utterance of their name draws their spirit from the afterlife. In the blackness of the night, when the owl calls, many shiver and tremble in the presence of such restless souls. Many fear, lest by careless talk they call back the dead.

But I did not.

When I looked upon the faces of my people as they went about their tasks, I realized there was a way I could learn the truth about my father's fate.

As night fell, across the camp there sounded the

rhythmic beat of a drum. The mournful voice of a singer pierced the gathering darkness.

My nerves quickened. Tonight the warriors would make the dance of war. I watched the tribes gather around the ceremonial fire, yet I stayed alone in the shadow of Dahtet's tepee.

I had my own purpose to fulfil this night.

In the distance, four masked figures approached the flames, coming into the light from the four directions, their faces marked with sacred pollen. As they began to dance and chant, their shadows were thrown high against the rock faces that ringed the plateau; it appeared that the mountains danced with them, and the night throbbed with their movement. Around the fire they swayed, and began to call the names of those who would fight against our Mexican enemies. They shouted for Golahka, and he stepped into the light, his lance borne aloft. With a warlike shout he began to weave and spin. More names were called, and more warriors joined the circle, waving their weapons with fierce passion, their loud war cries echoing from the rocks, so that the earth itself seemed to shriek for vengeance.

Power was strong in the Apache camp that night; it pulsed through the ground beneath my feet. It vibrated in the very air. I could smell it. Taste it. My fingertips pricked with the knowledge of it.

Golahka had once asked if I had Power.

On that night, it flowed through me.

I sat alone, and the masked dancers howled and spun and leapt in the firelight. As the Power grew I began to speak my father's name.

"Ashteh," I murmured. I would call him from the spirit world.

"Ashteh." His ghost would find his daughter.

"Ashteh." He would tell me of his terror.

"Ashteh." He would tell me of his death.

The night air took his name and drew it, quivering, from the living earth to the land of the spirits. I whispered his name again, over and over, my mouth forming the words in the rhythmic fervour of an incantation: "Ashteh, Ashteh, Ashteh. *Ashteh.*"

The smell of woodsmoke and sweat mingled with the scents of pine and sage. And all at once, the distant dancers blurred. The sound of their chanting faded and was no more. My heartbeat alone sounded in my ears, for it had begun to pound as rapidly as when returning from a mountain run, although I sat still unmoving. And then I ceased to hear even that. My mind loosed itself from my body and became as a breath in the night air. I was in a place where no line divides the living from the dead.

And yet he did not come forth to greet me.

Through that long night, over and over I invoked

113

my father. Yet his spirit did not walk. He did not haunt the plateau where we camped, and when at last uneasy sleep came to me, he did not find me in my dreams.

When I awoke, dread filled my belly, for dark suspicion – poisonous as the viper – had slithered into my mind. Perhaps my father had not come, because he could not.

It had been bitter sorrow to lose him. Yet now I feared a horror worse than the certainty of his death.

I feared my father lived.

At first light, the warriors came together in silence, their painted faces dotted with pollen, bands fixed tight across their brows. Each carried his own weapons, along with provisions for three days. We would kill game as we travelled, or we would go hungry, but we would not burden ourselves with more than this. All had tied a length of cloth about their waists to serve as clothing during the day, and to wrap themselves in at night. I, who was not yet a warrior, also took such weapons as I possessed, for I could not walk amongst our enemies unarmed. My bow and quiver I had slung across my back; my knife was at my waist; and Tazhi's spear hung, impatient, in my hand. And thus, when the chieftains led, we followed.

Towards Mexico.

The women and children watched solemnly, some moving their lips in fervent prayer to Ussen that their fathers, brothers, sons, would return safe. None prayed for me.

Huten saw our departure, his face an anguished mask. I would carry its image with me as we journeyed. I passed Dahtet, who looked upon me with her gentle eyes but spoke not. We had made an awkward farewell in the quiet of her tepee, both rueing the words that had passed between us that – though forgiven – could be neither unsaid nor forgotten.

Keste was the last, and as I walked by him he murmured so that none but I should hear, "Take care, Siki. Your father did not return from Mexico. Will you meet the same fate?"

His words chilled me, but I said nothing, for what answer could I give? I saw the wrath that burned within, and I did not wonder at Keste's sourness – I too would have known anger had I been asked to remain in the camp – but I feared how it would show itself to Dahtet in the absence of older, wiser men who might restrain him, and bid him hold his temper.

For all that day we walked: the Black Mountain, the Chokenne and the Dendhi Apache. We walked from sunrise to sunset, stopping only once to eat, following the hidden ways chosen by Golahka, along river beds and through ravines and mountains, where we would be concealed from our enemy.

And as we walked, in soft silence, I thought of my father.

None had ever found his body. Those who had survived the ambush had not lingered to retrieve and bury the dead. When he did not return, all had thought him slain. I had never until now questioned that certainty. For what but death would keep a warrior from his tribe? What but death would keep a husband from his wife? What but death would keep a father from his child?

My feet pounded the answers on the earth.

Shame.

Disgrace.

Treachery.

Before the sun sank beneath the horizon, the war party stopped in a river valley, beside a deep ravine where our fires could be safely lit without being seen. Should troops come upon us, the ravine gave us also the means by which we could escape and climb and conceal ourselves amongst the mountains.

Scouts were sent ahead to ensure no enemy was close by. The warriors sat down to rest and the novices set about their tasks. Mine was to collect firewood and thus I followed the river's course, for I had seen a line of trees that grew where the valley curved ahead and thought to begin my search there. But as I reached a bend in the river, I stopped suddenly. There before me lay a Mexican dwelling. Stone built, the rocks gouged from the body of Mother Earth, fenced with the hacked remains of felled trees.

I cursed my own foolishness. Blindly I had trusted our scouts, and once more I had wandered incautious. I dropped behind a rock, knowing that the Mexicans might yet come upon me, and slit my throat as easily as if I were a trapped rabbit. Even as I reached for my bow, I knew they might be drawing their weapons upon me. I recalled the death of the guards at Koskineh: slain before they had time to fire a single arrow.

And yet, even as my mind was flooded with such thoughts, I felt a pricking of the hairs upon my neck. All was not well in that place: the silence was too complete. The living, however still they may keep, however motionless they may stand, will fill a place with their presence. A human soul will quiver and set the air around it trembling. That dwelling did not contain living people – I was sure of it.

I stole a look over the rock that hid me, and let out a long breath of relief. It was deserted. Warily I approached, my bow strung with an arrow lest any came upon me. As I neared the doorway, a startled kid goat ran out and I loosed my arrow, piercing her between the ribs. She slumped against the drunken door and, leaving her where she lay, I stepped over her and entered the dwelling.

It was the first time I had seen inside the house of a Mexican, and to my eyes it was a strange and curious sight. The Apache moves upon the land lightly, leaving few signs of his passing. For firewood he picks what has fallen; to make a brushwood shelter he ties small saplings together. If he must cut wood, he takes but little from the living tree. Not so the Mexican, who hews and hacks and gouges to force the earth to his will. Much labour had been expended in the building of the dwelling, and yet I wondered how its inhabitants could have borne to remain there, for the place was dark as a cave. The air was thick and sour; the wind could not breathe freely. None who lived there could glimpse the wide sky, nor look upon the stars. To live within must be daily torment.

Many objects – whose purpose I could not divine – littered the beaten earth floor. The figure of a tortured man, nailed by hands and feet to crossed branches, hung upon the stone wall. I shuddered at the barbarity of the image. A man must walk in the afterlife with his body in the same condition as it has left the living earth. This man must walk for ever with maimed hands and broken feet. How could any bear to look upon such suffering?

My eye was caught by a red and black coloured blanket; Tehineh had laid her babe upon such a one as this. It had been chewed in one corner by the goat. I reached towards it, and as my fingers stroked the woven threads Power filled me, and my mind ran free with images.

I know not how I saw it. It was not as clear as watching a reflection dancing upon the water, nor yet so indistinct as a blurred, half-forgotten memory. Power flooded me with the knowledge that a black-haired man had once dwelt here, with his wife and child.

Riders came, Chokenne warriors, who sought meat to fill the bellies of their children. The land had been theirs long before the coming of the Mexican. Why should they hunger amid this plenty? His eyes brimful of outrage, the black-haired man ran to stop the Chokenne freeing his animals. A warrior swung his club and the black-haired man was slain. The woman fled, the babe clutched to her breast. For a fleeting moment she had the look of Tehineh as she ran. The warriors watched her go. They were kinder than those who had ridden against our women and children at Koskineh and did not pursue.

I dropped the blanket and stood, as startled by the occurrence of the vision as by its content. My breath came in sharp gasps. I steadied myself, and felt the sudden need to get away from that place, to be amongst my own people once more.

Heaving the goat around my neck, I returned to our camp; the warriors would welcome the taste of fresh meat. I told none of what I had seen, although Chee saw the shock upon my face and raised his eyebrows in enquiry. I did not speak, for I was a novice and would keep my silence. Pushing the troubling images away and leaving Chee to skin the goat, I pursued my task of gathering wood.

And as I did so, I cursed that Ussen should have given me Power, and that I, in using it, had felt for the black-haired Mexican – my enemy! – nothing but pity.

From sunrise to sunset on each day that we walked I thought of Koskineh, only Koskineh. I threaded the memories of that slaughter like beads onto a sinew thread, and wore them around my neck as an amulet.

I saw the mother of Golahka, felled like brushwood. Slender Tehineh, blood blooming on her deerskin shirt. Her children – the children of Golahka – hacked to pieces.

And Tazhi, who even now walked the spirit world, maimed and broken.

I knew not how many days we walked thus. The rigours of the journey and the tasks I had to perform as novice tested my body as it had never been tested before. Many miles we walked each day, and the work was hard and heavy when we made camp. Because we also had to stand guard, I had little time to be refreshed with sleep. In addition I had to remember the many rules Golahka had spoken of: I should not gaze upwards at the sky, lest I invite heavy rain to fall upon us; if I had to look backwards I should turn following the direction of the sun. Many times I feared I would endanger the war party by forgetting the many strictures and prohibitions governing a novice's behaviour.

But at last, as the sun began to sink and colour the earth red with its dying rays, we halted and made camp on the hills that rose behind the town of Jujio. And now we concealed neither our force nor our intent. As we looked down upon the dwellings of our enemies I smelt the scent of fear drift upon the evening air. The Mexicans quaked at the sight of us, and I rejoiced in their terror. I gazed at the town for long moments. In that place were the men who had ridden against us; in that place were their loved ones.

There lived the man who had slain Tazhi.

I turned away, and set about my tasks. As I began to gather wood, my palms grew suddenly hot, and tingled as if bitten by ants. I dropped the branch I held, and spoke aloud.

"They come," I said. "Eight men. They come to talk."

I was a novice; I was not to speak unless asked to do so. Punte opened his mouth to chide me for my impudence, but Golahka, who was close by, stopped him. He seized me by the arm, and said, "Mexicans? You are sure? You have seen it?"

I nodded. I knew not how, but I was as certain they came as if I had watched them take their horses from their stables and place the saddles upon their backs.

And as Golahka fixed me with his blackly glinting eyes, a scout who watched the town called, "Riders!"

Golahka smiled at me grimly and nodded with satisfaction, for he had proved himself right: he thought I had Power, and it was so.

Eight soldiers wearing the dark clothes I had seen at Koskineh rode into our camp, carrying the white flag of truce. As I looked up at their faces, rage flared within me. They had slaughtered the defenceless. The unarmed. Children. Babes. Had I

122

held Tazhi's spear in my hand as they climbed down from their horses and smiled coldly upon our chief I would have used it.

Chodini did not smile. He raised his hand, and the order was given.

Swiftly the eight were captured. Cleanly were they killed. Flint-sharp knives were drawn across their throats and the first blood of the Apache revenge was spilt on Mexican soil. We had not come to talk. Battle was all we sought. Killing the men thus would draw the troops from the town to a place of our choosing.

By dawn, they would come.

The crowing of a bird marked the new day. Three times its harsh call pierced the air, as the sky began to lighten in the east. And from the town terror rose like the shimmering haze of desert heat. I felt the women's dread; I knew their longing to hold the darkness, to slow the moon's set, to bid the sun pause awhile. But they could not stop this day – a day that would bring death to many – from dawning.

I had not slept, for I along with all the novices had kept watch during the long night while the warriors took their rest. In truth, I did not think many of them slept deeply. Though our force was great, the Mexican troops numbered more. Throughout the camp was the knowledge that the fight to come would be long and hard.

Golahka called the warriors to council.

"We shall deceive our enemy," he told them, and briefly his black eyes met mine. "For I have seen that often cunning will prevail where strength may not."

The town of Jujio stands on a wide plain, and is backed by rolling hills. These are cleft by a broad river valley that runs from north to south before it meets the plain. Golahka directed half the warriors to remain with him in the valley, beside the river with their backs to the hills, in the cover of the brush and trees. They were ill hidden, and thus it was intended. To a Mexican eye it would look as though our whole force held the ground in that one place. Golahka gave orders that the rest of the men should go quietly across the flat valley, and conceal themselves in the facing hills.

We novices were advised to remain apart, high on a peak, where we would be safe. We were to keep out of danger, and stay far from the battle so that we should not impede the warriors in their task. If the fight was lost and the warriors had to flee, we were to go at once to the appointed place and wait there until we could regroup. It made much sense. But I could no more follow this advice than stop the sun from rising.

I crept down the hill to a place from where I could watch the battle, and Chee crept beside me, for how could we do otherwise? I knew not where Ishta and Naite went, but I was certain they would not remain in the place of safety. Chee and I concealed ourselves below the breast of a sharp outcrop, at the foot of which ran the river that divided us from where Golahka stood with his force. We dared creep no closer. But from here I could watch all. If Tazhi's slayer came, I would see him.

We waited the long, weary morning. Not until the sun was high did the Mexican soldiers march from the town. Our warriors in the river valley gave a great war cry as the scouts passed word of the advancing troops, but the warriors hidden amongst the hills kept still and silent. No eye would detect their presence there. They had vanished into the land like the sweet spring rain.

The Mexicans marched into the valley. Two columns of soldiers on foot, with a great crowd more of men on horseback held in reserve. I looked upon the Mexican commander with astonishment; he kept well behind his troops, where he was in no danger. No Apache chief would behave thus. A chief goes ahead of his warriors into battle; he is first in any attack: how else can he claim to be their leader? I marvelled at the cowardice of this Mexican, who ordered his men forward – driving them before him like cattle – while he himself sat on his great warhorse and did not fight.

As the Mexicans advanced, the earth pulsed with the beat of many feet marching together in perfect unity. It was a strange manner of warfare to me. When they had come but halfway across the valley floor, they stopped and stood in lines – easy targets for our warriors. As bowstrings twanged and the air hissed with the flight of many Apache arrows, the Mexicans opened fire.

The first wave of shots hit the cover where our warriors stood in less time than it takes to blink. And in that time, many fell, to rise no more. Jotah, father of Huten, who had broken the silence with his laughter after our deer hunt, was amongst those slain.

A second line of Mexicans stepped forward and fired, and more of my people fell lifeless to the earth. The gun seemed a terrible thing to me then: it slaughtered without skill, without honour. The clumsiest, most cowardly man could kill with it as well as the finest of warriors. Despair like a cold hand clutched at my belly.

But even as it sank, my heart rose once more.

With a mighty cry – a sound born of the raging grief that enveloped his heart – Golahka charged at the Mexican lines. Shots rained down upon him, but it seemed the great hand of Ussen shielded him from their fire. The warriors, fierce in their warpaint, the lust for blood gleaming in their eyes, followed where Golahka led. Terror swept through the Mexican troops. Frantically their leader called upon them, but from where he sat his soldiers could not hear such orders as he gave. And as Golahka charged, the warriors who had been concealed in the hills behind the Mexicans now showed themselves and ran, whooping, down upon them.

The straight lines of the Mexican forces were broken, and now each man had to face his enemy and fight one to one. Golahka moved as if he could not be harmed; his battle fury was relentless and many, many Mexicans fell at his hand. As each soldier thudded to the earth, Golahka stripped him of his gun, throwing it to those of the Chokenne who knew how to use such a weapon. Thus was their leader slain – shot by a musket taken from one of his own men.

The battle was swift, the fighting desperate. The heated air turned rank with the tang of gunpowder, sweat and blood. Our warriors fell, lying stiff upon Mexican soil. In the time it takes to butcher a deer, the battle was nearly over.

Those who remained of our force were bunched together by the river. But Golahka, who had been at the heart of the fight, stood with three others in the centre of a field strewn with corpses.

Two soldiers were galloping towards them.

I saw with sick fear that Golahka's arrows were gone, and the lances of his fellow warriors had long since been buried in the breasts of Mexicans. They could fight only with knives and their hands. As the soldiers rode at them, firing their guns, two warriors fell. Golahka and the remaining warrior ran towards the river. A Mexican sword cut down Golahka's companion before they could get there.

But now Golahka had reached our own men. Seizing a lance from the hand of Punte, he turned. The Mexican pointed his gun at the heart of the great warrior. But – perhaps nudged by the great hand of Ussen – his horse stumbled. The shot missed its mark.

Golahka did not. With a mighty cry he thrust the lance, and the rider fell at his feet. Taking the sword from this dead Mexican's hand, Golahka used it against the second rider. He leapt at the soldier, slicing his arm and pulling him from his horse. They both fell upon the ground, grappling in the dust.

Then there was a terrible stillness, and both lay motionless. The very earth seemed to hold its breath.

But Golahka had slain his enemy. His knife had found the throat of the Mexican, who lay still, pinning him to the ground. With a heaving roll, Golahka was up once more, brandishing the sword, looking for more soldiers that he might kill.

There were none. The whole of the Mexican force lay dead.

The exultant Apache cry of victory rang in the valley, echoing from hill to hill, until the air shook with our triumph. It could not bring Tehineh back from the afterlife, nor his mother and children. Yet glory was Golahka's, and he joyed in his vengeance.

Slipping at once from where Chee and I had hidden ourselves, without waiting for him to join me, I hastened towards the field of battle. I crept down the rocky outcrop with silent speed: moving with caution had been a lesson I would not lightly forget.

Reaching the foot of the rock face, I paused. And it was then that I saw the man who had killed my brother.

He knelt, concealed from the battlefield by the rock around which I viewed him. And as he knelt, he took his musket and fed it with a single shot, ramming it home with a length of metal. From the care he took, I judged it to be his last. He looked towards Golahka, who stood, heady with battle joy, amongst the warriors. Golahka, who had terrorized the Mexican force.

Golahka, who had led our warriors to great victory. Golahka, whom this man was determined to kill.

Tazhi's spear grew hot in my palm. It thrilled with the desire for blood. To use it, I must face him. Face him, and use my brother's spear without hesitation. I edged forward a finger's breadth. As I moved, the Mexican took aim upon Golahka.

Yet he did not fire. For Chodini too had moved, and now stood before his finest warrior – in the line the shot would fly – and this man wanted to spend the last of his ammunition on none but Golahka. He lowered his gun, shaking his head in frustration.

Just then Chee came sliding down the scree beside me, laughing with the delight of our victory.

With one swift leap the Mexican was above us, standing on the rock that had concealed him, his gun loaded, his sword at his belt. He was torn between firing upon us, and firing upon Golahka. But he looked down on me and saw a child. A girl child of no consequence, who held nothing but a small spear – a plaything. Beside her, a youth. Both unimportant. Insignificant.

He lifted his musket to his shoulder, took aim upon Golahka and fired. But not before I had swung the shaft of Tazhi's spear, knocking his arm and spoiling his shot. Incensed, he threw his gun to the dusty earth and drew his sword.

I spoke Tazhi's name aloud. In that moment, I called him – maimed as he was – from the spirit world. The air quivered with his presence. Tazhi stood beside me when I avenged him.

The Mexican smiled upon me. He laughed.

And then he lifted his sword.

Tazhi's spear burned in my hand. With the swiftness of the wind that had run in my brother's veins, I drove it into the breast of the Mexican. Easily, softly, as if guided by Ussen, the sharp head slid between his ribs and found his heart.

A gunshot is not silent. All had turned at its sound. All had watched the Mexican fall, Tazhi's spear buried in his chest. All had witnessed my vengeance.

Clenching my teeth against the sudden cold that seized me, I pulled Tazhi's spear from the heart of his slayer and went to wash it clean in the shallow river that wound through that valley. As I plunged my bloodied hands into the fast-flowing water, I felt again Power course through me.

The water ran darkly, and in it I saw another Mexican dwelling. A woman was there; the same woman I had seen flee with her babe clutched to her breast. But now she lay slain, her skull split wide, her blood spilt upon the floor. A Chokenne warrior held her child fast in his arms. He took the babe from the dwelling and placed him upon his horse, riding far away into the sloping hills.

The water ran clear once more, and the darkness became naught but the stony bed of the river. I was left standing knee-deep in the cold torrent, wondering at the meaning of what Ussen had shown me.

Following the heated thrill of battle came great weariness. It crept amongst the warriors, bringing heavy silence upon them. Yet none could rest; there was much to be done before we could turn our faces for home.

Kinsmen took the bodies of their dead, carrying them away for burial in secret places. Chee and I moved amongst the slain Mexicans, gathering weapons. Golahka and Chodini reasoned that if the Mexicans were armed with guns, then so must we be. The Black Mountain Apache had to master this weapon, and master it swiftly, if we were to defend ourselves against further attacks. As I plucked the gleaming gun from the hand of a dead man, I saw that more attacks would come, as surely as dark night must follow bright day.

I knew the women of the town quaked; the children wept in dread of what the Apache might do to them. If it had been possible to quench their fear, I would have done so. But I had no words of the

Spanish tongue to tell them that this was not our way. We would not ride against the powerless, the unarmed. Our fight had been with the men, the soldiers who had ridden barbarously against our people; the women and children of Jujio would be left unharmed. Silently I pitied their sorrow, even as I gloried in our victory.

Taking only such things as we needed – horses, swords, guns, ammunition – we began our journey homewards. We divided into many small bands so that pursuit, if it came, would be made difficult. Sotchez rode north through the river valley; Toah took his men east across the hills; Ozheh, son of Chodini, took a route that curved first to the south; I followed Chodini and Golahka across the broad plain, heading north when we reached the hills.

It was agreed that the bands would meet at the foot of the mountain plateau where our people camped; thus we would enter the settlement together in triumph for the feast of victory. Our scouts went swiftly by the shortest way that they might give the women news of our coming.

As we rode beside a winding river towards the distant hills, I thought Golahka seemed little relieved by his revenge. Battle lust had drained him, and left a tired, brooding warrior who sat silent in his saddle, his loathing of the Mexican unquenched.

For my own part, I joyed in my vengeance. I could neither ease Tazhi's passage through the afterlife, nor wipe away the horror of his perpetual mutilation, but the weight of pain I had long carried was a little lightened by the justice of my act. Yet I also feared what lay ahead, for well I knew that word of my triumph would inflame Keste's enmity still further.

Of the visions Ussen had shown me, I thought less, for I could make no sense of them. I did not wish to feel pity for the Mexican, nor did I wish to learn what lay in his mind: such knowledge weakened me. I was to be a warrior. A warrior must have no weakness. Thus I pushed the images aside, and shut my heart against them.

The land we traversed opened into a broad valley, where tall cottonwoods swayed, graceful beside a fast-flowing river. There Chodini pulled his horse to a sudden halt.

There, in that tranquil vale, where the wind rippled the leaves and the sunlight danced on the water, I first looked upon the face of a white man.

They were camped beside the river. Soldiers, all dressed in the same garb. Five men, with hair as yellow as the sun-dried grass and skin of a strange, light hue. When I saw their eyes, my breath came in a sharp gasp.

The eyes of the Apache are dark throughout: at the centre a dot of black is circled with deepest brown and the eye is edged with the soft buff of deerskin. But the centres of these men's eyes were circled with the blue of the wide sky and edged with the shocking white of sun-bleached bone.

Chodini urged his horse forward, and as he approached he smiled and raised his hand in greeting. The men came forward to meet him, and our chief swung down from his saddle.

"Welcome, strangers to the great land of the Apache."

Our chief spoke in Spanish and in Spanish the men replied; it was the only common tongue, for Chodini knew none of the White Eyes' language and they spoke no Apache.

"We come in friendship," said the yellow-haired leader. "And in peace. We seek a small corner where we may live quietly with our brothers."

Chodini held his arms wide as if indicating the extent of Ussen's creation. "Our land is broad. Make your homes here. Mother Earth can provide for us all."

For a little while the men stood and talked with our chief. Chodini warned them to be wary; amongst these mountains were known to be renegade bands of Apache – wild young men who put themselves beyond the jurisdiction of their chiefs. The strangers seemed little troubled by this information; they were well weaponed and could defend themselves.

And so, with hands clasped all swore brotherhood. Such words are binding to an Apache: these men would suffer no harm from my tribe.

It was a pleasant exchange – a meeting that promised warmth and friendship between our peoples – and yet as Chodini mounted once more, I felt fear trickle coolly down my spine. It was as if I had passed into a dark cave where the sun's rays could not warm the air. Once before I had felt this sensation, and then the chill had come from the hate-filled eyes of Keste. Now I looked about me for its source, but could see nothing.

We rode on, and as we passed, the White Eyes smiled in perfect amity, their faces bearing expressions of openness and honesty. I had no reason to feel as I did, and was startled by the strangeness of my sudden dread. I told myself it was mere fancy, and yet unease pursued me like the wolf who slips from shadow to shadow.

At the head of the valley, the trail wound sharply and the land began to rise. I rode at the rear of our party. Before we passed out of sight of the strangers' encampment, I chanced to look back. Had my eyes not been so sharp, I might perhaps have missed the small, furtive movement of a man within the tent.

A sixth man. A man who had remained hidden when Chodini extended his vow of friendship. A man who had not come forward to clasp hands and bond in brotherhood with our people. His hand held to his forehead to shade his eyes from the sun, he looked in the direction of our party of warriors. When he saw we were not yet all gone from view, he withdrew swiftly back into the tent.

It was not his covert movement alone that set my nerves jangling. What alarmed me more was the colour of his hair. The five pale-skinned strangers were yellow-headed. This man was dark. As dark-haired as a Mexican. Or an Apache.

We met the rest of our war party in the appointed place and returned to our settlement as the sun sank low in the sky. The women knew of our approach and already the fires were burning in readiness for the feast to come. As we rode upwards along the precipitous path to our tepees the distant smell of woodsmoke was a sweet balm to my senses.

We came in triumph, and yet full well I knew that our homecoming would bring raw sorrow to many.

I rode behind the war party but I could feel the excitement from the camp, where I knew a row of eager boys would be waiting, desperate to attract attention to themselves. It is a fine thing to be noticed by a warrior returning from the warpath: to be handed his horse to tend is a great honour, and boys fought amongst themselves for the positions where they would most likely be seen. As a novice, I would tend my horse myself, and thus when I rode into our camp the line of boys had already dispersed, and become instead a noisy swarm that buzzed after the warriors, eager for tales of battle.

Chee, Ishta and Naite had gone before me, and were now embraced by their mothers as they slid from their horses, with muttered words of thanks to Ussen for their safe return. There was no one waiting for me. I glanced about in search of Dahtet; I had a strong wish to see her gentle face, and I thought she might perhaps have come to give me welcome. Not seeing her, I felt a rush of sadness, but reasoned that she must be occupied in preparations for the feast. I would go and seek her later, but first I had to look to my horse.

I dismounted and began to check her over. It was only when the animal started, half rearing and snorting with alarm, that I realized I was not, after all, alone. A boy was in the shadows, so still that in the half-light I had not been aware of his presence. A boy who was rooted to the earth, immobile and stiff as the stone mountains that circled the camp. A boy whose face was stricken with shock and grief.

Huten.

He had seen the warriors return. One by one they had passed him. Jotah, his father, had not been amongst them. And even as I stood watching him, the death wail of his mother and sister rang across the camp. They were joined by others as news of our losses spread, and the darkening sky was pierced with the terrible sounds of lamentation. The cries stirred Huten and without a word he began to stagger, like one mortally injured, towards his tepee.

My chest ached, for I knew how deeply the women and children of Jujio would also be mourning, and to me it seemed that the whole land was smothered by a huge cloud of anguish. I rested my head against the mare's neck, and drew what little comfort I could from the animal. Then, freeing her to the herd, I went in search of Dahtet.

I could not find her. With growing unease I sought throughout the camp. I looked where Kaywin, wife of Toah, stood magnificent in beaded buckskin robes directing preparations for the feast. I searched where the women were spreading a great half-circle of skins and blankets upon the ground. I walked amongst those who filled jugs with tiswin – the drink the Apache relish in times of celebration – and those who tended the fires, and laid strips of meat and sweet acorn cakes to roast.

I did not see Dahtet, but at last I saw her mother, Hosidah. When I spoke her daughter's name, Hosidah's eyes met mine, but almost at once she cast down her head, and gave a small shake as if she did not want me to approach. In the glowing light her face was a grim mask and my heart contracted with sudden fear. I paused, wondering what I should do. I sorely wished to have news of Dahtet. But then the chiefs emerged from their tepees dressed in their finery and all questions would have to wait.

Singers and drummers took their places. By firelight Chodini, Toah and Sotchez led the line of warriors to the feast. The men sat upon the skins, each according to his rank and deeds of battle. Last came those who had completed their fourth raid, and were new made as warriors. Naite walked amongst them, his eyes cast down in humility, but with a broad smile creasing the corners of his mouth which he could not suppress. His father, Naichise, brother to Chodini, sat upright, his lips pressed tight together to conceal his proud delight. Naite settled himself upon the ground, and then the novices took their places. I was to sit in front of Chee, for though this was but the first time I had journeyed with the warriors, my act of vengeance had given me higher status. Once we were seated, however, I edged back until I was beside him, for I thought to question him of Dahtet as soon as I had the opportunity. The women and children settled themselves in rows behind us.

Food had already been taken silently to families who did not join the celebration: those who had lost a husband, a brother, a father, kept to their tepees. When all were served, Chodini lit an oak leaf rolled with tobacco and blew smoke in the four directions. Then, raising his cup of tiswin, our feast began.

141

At once I spoke to Chee. "I cannot find Dahtet."

Between mouthfuls of strong, sweet meat, Chee spoke words that turned the food sour in my mouth.

"Keste would not stay to guard the women," he murmured. "It is said he felt shamed by Chodini's words – shamed beyond enduring. And so he left. The sunset that followed our departure he went from the camp, secretly, in the dark."

"And Dahtet went with him?"

Chee nodded.

We were silent while we considered the rashness of his deed. Shame is horror indeed for the Apache, and to lose face will cause more intense and lasting pain to a warrior than any hurt to the body. Well I understood how hard Keste had found it to endure. And yet I felt with rising anger that he *should* have endured it. To leave the tribe – to go willingly from the protection and fellowship of his brothers – was an act of utter folly. No words from Chodini or Golahka could shame him as much as he had now shamed himself. Ignominy would be heaped upon his name. He had made himself a renegade, an outcast. And worse – much worse – he had carried Dahtet into exile.

Even as I rued the loss of her, I began to wonder if she had gone willingly.

"Is it said that Keste forced her from the can..." I asked.

Chee shook his head. "I do not know. None saw them go. But, Siki, her fondness for Keste was no secret."

He spoke truth. Dahtet's love had burnt beyond sense, beyond reason. I had to yield that it might, perhaps, have severed her from her people. And yet the thought did not lie quietly in my breast.

"She was a loving daughter. Mindful, always, of her duty. She would not lightly have caused her parents shame. And now she is dead to them."

Chee acknowledged that it was so.

"She wished for marriage," I continued, speaking the thoughts freely as they ran through my mind. "Honourable marriage. Keste had only to ride on one more raid before he could wed her. Proudly she would have stood beside him as his wife. She desired her parents to look on and approve her match, of that I am certain. I do not think Dahtet walked willingly into such disgrace."

"Perhaps you are right, Siki," said Chee. "It may be that Keste deceived her into banishment. But I doubt we shall ever know the truth."

With a heavy heart, I agreed. Dahtet was an outcast: it was impossible that we would meet again. I must mourn for her as another one dead.

*　*　*

When we had eaten, Chodini stood, and all fell silent to hear him. In a low voice he named the warriors who had died in battle. "Our honoured dead are fortunate. They died for their tribe. They have gone before us to the Happy Place. Let them not be disturbed. From this day, let not their names be spoken." A murmur of assent – of farewell – rippled around the listeners.

And then from the darkness, boys led forth horses heavily laden with guns and ammunition that we had brought with us from Mexico. These were distributed to those who had need of them. Each chief made sure his people were well supplied. They took naught for themselves, as is the way of an Apache leader. Although I had requested nothing, I found Golahka placing a sleekly shining musket in my hands, and sprinkling ammunition into my lap. My heart leapt with joy that the great warrior should bestow such honour on me, and I lifted my eyes to his. No smile answered mine. Rather his eyes seemed to flash with irritation as he noticed where I sat beside Chee. In not heeding the ritual of the feast and staying in my position I had shown disrespect, and I thought this irked him for he moved past without a word.

I sat fingering the cold metal of my gun. I was full

aware that it was an accolade, a tribute, and I was grateful for it. And yet I disliked the weapon. To me it seemed a spiritless thing. I hoped never to have need of it.

After the distribution of supplies, it was Golahka's turn to speak. He gave an account of the battle and detailed the valiant exploits of those who had excelled. Of me, he said, "This girl has avenged her brother. It was well done. Much honour is due to Siki."

Approving whispers spread from mouth to mouth. An aged Chokenne warrior, his face so withered that the bones gleamed through his skin, tilted his head towards me in a gesture of respect. It seemed I had passed from being a strange oddity to being one who was held in high esteem. Flushed with triumph, I fixed my eyes on the ground before me. I could not help but feel pride glow in my heart; there was great delight in being praised thus. Once more, I raised my chin to look at Golahka, and saw him staring back at me. But his eyes did not glory in his pupil's achievement as I had expected; instead he looked searchingly at my face, as if he sought to know the secrets I kept hidden. Under his burning scrutiny, I felt my soul begin to blister, even as the sage leaf had once seared my flesh.

Scalded, my eyes recoiled from his, and came to rest instead on another's face.

Punte, father of Keste.

A chill stab pierced the night air between us. He veiled his expression at once, and sat gazing blankly back at me. But for that one unguarded moment, I had seen his heart. It was brimful of fury.

For many days our tribes remained feasting together on the high plateau. Our victory had been great, and thus our celebrations were long and joyful. New-made warriors strode amongst the tepees full of delighted, youthful pride. To be a full warrior was also to be a man, and some who had discreetly courted before our journey now took new wives into their tepees. Some older warriors – whose skills at hunting allowed them to support more than one wife – took the widows of those who had been slain at Jujio under their protection. There is little ceremony to an Apache marriage: it is a private thing, arranged between families, and any celebrations became part of the general feasting.

A warrior should be married, and yet Golahka continued to walk alone, his face still darkened by the ache of his family's loss. He did not join the men in their racing and gambling, but instead learnt mastery of the gun. The mountain air was split with its noise, sending birds into flight, and children shrieking to their mothers.

* * *

I had had my fill – and more – of weapons and war-fare. In the warm sunshine, I wished to feed awhile on lightness and joy.

There is a game the Apache play in times of peace, and this we did now. On a flat, grassy space at the far end of the plateau a group of men and boys gath-ered for shinny. Few women were there, for their hands were kept busy with preparing food, although the fleetest of foot had cast aside their tasks, unable to resist the draw of the game. I was amongst them, standing beside Chee, hoping to be chosen.

Torrez, father of Ishta, was leader of one team; Dhezi – a Chokenne warrior – his opponent. They each selected five of the swiftest or strongest amongst us to join on their teams. Happy was I to be chosen by Torrez, and I took my curved stick of oak in readiness for the game's commencement.

Chee was picked for the opposing team, and he pointed his stick at me as if firing a gun. "Today we are enemies, Siki," he said, his eyes gleaming with humour. "Let the battle begin."

"You are slow as the frost-dulled snake," I replied in the same tone. "You shall be left eating dust while I run."

"You think so?" he said. "And what will you chance to prove yourself right?"

147

Thus it was, in jest with Chee, that I came to gamble my quiver full of arrows on the outcome of the game.

Those who watched withdrew to the cover of the trees, standing by the saplings at either end of the field that marked our goals. Torrez spat on a flat stone and threw it high in the air.

"Wet!" he called, and indeed the stone fell to earth with its wet side up. Thus Torrez chose which goal his team would aim for. It was morning, and he decided to defend the one the sun was yet rising behind, so that our opponents would have to run into its glare.

All spread wide across the grass. Ishta and Naite were there, as well as Zazuah and Kayitah, both fine Chokenne warriors. We faced our enemies: Chee; Chico, from whose ears dangled decorations of feather and turquoise; Toro; Pocito, in whose tepee I had lain when I tracked Golahka to the Chokenne camp; and Asha, a Dendhi woman of great swiftness and agility who had lately become wife to Chico.

The game commenced. The two leaders stood, their linked sticks raised in the centre of the field. Throwing the buckskin ball high into the air, Dhezi struck it hard on its descent, and sent it spinning through the air towards Chee.

Thereafter, everything was noise and mayhem. To kick the ball is permitted, and also to strike it with the curved stick, but to touch it with one's hands is not allowed. Sticks are used not only to beat the ball, but also freely against an opponent.

I was of smaller stature than the others, and so I skirted the edge of the play and the slashing sticks, watching for my chance to strike the ball. But before I had managed it even once, Chee's rapid flight ended in the first goal of the game.

"Your quiver is lost!" he called to me mockingly.

"I think not," I shouted back. "The game has scarce begun."

With smiles of triumph Chee's teammates spread once more across the field. The two leaders returned to the middle, and threw the ball high. Once more, Dhezi was swifter, and struck the ball towards Asha. With small tapping hits, she kept it close and thus was able to manoeuvre around Ishta and Naite. Once through the pack of players she struck hard and passed the ball to Chee, who was near the goal.

But Zazuah, hooking his curved stick around Chee's ankle, toppled him and seized the ball. A flick with his toes, and it was airborne. He struck it with his oak stick and it flew high and wide. Towards me. The ball's arcing path was such that it would have flown beyond the grassy pitch and landed amongst the tepees, but I leapt high to intercept it, turning as I jumped and sending it towards the goal.

My legs started to run even before I had come back down upon the earth, and as I landed I sped after the ball, kicking it hard as it thudded to the grass. Once, twice more, I struck, and rapidly came upon the goal, well ahead of my opponents. Toro alone blocked my path, his girth as broad as the rump of a bull.

Solid he was, but not swift. Copying Asha's way of hitting the ball with small taps, I kept it close. Looking to one side of him, I made as if to pass that way. As he began to move, I dodged to his other side and hurled the ball between the shaded trees to the triumphant shouts from my team.

I was not permitted such a free run again. There was much whispering amongst the opposing team as Torrez and Dhezi returned to the middle of the pitch, and as the ball was thrown into the air, I found myself with Chico at my side hounding me as closely as if he were my shadow. While I was thus pursued, Chee's team scored two more goals.

It seemed the only way to evade Chico was by entering the mass of players who surged towards the sunlit goal in pursuit of Chee and Dhezi. As I passed Pocito, I stepped in front of him, and to avoid falling over me Pocito jumped to one side, straight into Chico's path. He tripped, and both warriors tumbled headlong into the grass. Ahead of me, Torrez tackled Chee and took control of the ball. He hurled it to me over the heads of the players, and once more I broke free.

I ran towards the shadows. Toro stood before me. I dodged but he was not to be deceived again. With a savage blow he struck my shins, and I fell, rolling far across the grass. The other players now crashed upon Toro like a herd of horses. All was sweat and confusion, entwined limbs, knotted sticks, and the ball was nowhere to be seen.

Then I spotted it from where I lay, winded, upon the ground at some distance from the throng. It was between the feet of Toro, at the centre of the mass of struggling players. Chico's ear ornaments were wound in Pocito's hair; Chee was caught on Ishta's stick. All fought for freedom. Crawling forward, I slid my stick along the ground between their legs, and hooked the ball free from the pack. I hurled it between the trees before the others had loosed themselves from their entanglement.

The crowd shrieked with laughter. Amongst that great noise, I heard a familiar voice, and looked to see Golahka, who stood watching, his black eyes dancing with amusement. Joy it was to see him smile, and to hear him call, "Ah, Siki, your ways are ever distinct. Never have I seen shinny played upon the belly!"

*   *   *

The game continued long, with players growing
ever wearier. By the time the sun stood high in the
sky, and Kayitah's nose had been bloodied with
a blow from Toro's stick, Torrez and Dhezi called
the game to its finish. We had lost the match; and
now, with good humour, all settled their wagers. I
rued that I had not made a smaller bet with Chee;
to hand him the quiver I had laboured so hard over
was a great loss. But he had won them fairly, and
claimed them with a smile. Thus carelessly did I
deprive myself of my arrows without a moment's
real unease. I was amongst my kinsmen. What need
had I of weapons?

After some days, our tribes divided and went their
separate ways. But before our camp was struck, a
Chokenne woman came to me, and asked, "You are
Siki?"

I acknowledged that it was so.

"I am Paso. Danzih, my father, would wish to
speak with you."

I was puzzled, but followed the woman as she
led the way, winding between the tepees of the
Chokenne.

An aged man sat awaiting my arrival, and at once
I recognized him as the Chokenne warrior who had

nodded his approval at our victory feast. He was so ancient that it seemed his bones strained towards the air as though they longed to shed their fleshy burden. Such skin as remained upon his person hung in many folds, as dry and brittle as oak leaves in autumn.

And yet the man's eyes burned bright when he spoke. "Siki?" he asked. "You are daughter to Ashteh?"

I nodded, greatly surprised that he spoke my father's name. Perhaps the old man did not fear to draw forth restless spirits for he walked so near to death himself that dwellers of the afterlife held no terror for him.

Or perhaps he knew my father to be alive.

I sat beside him, eager to know why he had summoned me. And the man with the face of death stretched his thin lips in a smile and reached for me. He pulled me towards him and, tracing the line of my jaw with a withered finger, he laughed.

"Siki," he said. "You are so like your father. I am glad to have this chance to see his daughter. Well I knew him as a boy. He was playmate to my son; I watched them grow to manhood together. They were close as blood-born brothers." He sighed. "How proud your father would have been of your triumph."

He did not need to tell me his own son was dead. I saw in the moisture that fast swelled and beaded in the corners of his eyes that he mourned his loss.

In a cracked dry whisper he began to tell me stories of my father's boyhood. Good stories. Apache stories. Stories that made me smile. He told of my father's fierceness in wrestling; his swiftness and fleetness of foot; his agility on horseback; his fearless bravado; how he had spent much time crawling upon his belly, creeping thus upon his playmates that he might startle them into screaming – just as I had once done. And yet the one thing I longed to know he did not speak of.

At last – lacking in courtesy though it was – I could not stop the words spilling from my mouth. "Does my father live?"

The old man looked at me with great astonishment. I saw then that his intention had been but to reminisce, to recall fondly a past that had gone. He looked as if I had lifted my hand and struck him.

He shook his head firmly. "No, Siki. In this you are wrong. Ashteh is dead."

But his hands had begun to shake, and a pulse throbbed at his temple. I thought he kept something from me, and so I persisted. "You cannot be certain."

"I can, Siki, my child. Indeed I can."

"No. I called his name. His spirit did not come. He lives." I would not let the matter rest but recklessly pursued it, until the old man was forced to speak words that cut me to the heart.

His voice dropped to a whisper. "Your father is dead. Of this there can be no doubt. Siki... It was I who found him."

With trembling hands, he reached into the pouch at his waist, and pulled forth a length of sinew, beaded with turquoise and silver. He placed the beads in my hands. I saw at once it was the necklet my mother had fashioned and hung around the neck of my beloved father to keep him from harm. It had been his amulet, his most precious token.

"His bones had been picked clean by beasts," the old man said. "It was by this necklet I knew him. I took it so that none may know him. I buried his body in a hidden place, that none may find him."

As I fingered the turquoise, I recalled the anguished face of my mother. She had spent many moons watching, waiting, hoping for my father's return. We had never heard his fate.

"But why did you not tell us? Why did you not bring word of his death?" I asked.

It was then that the old man's voice cracked with pain. His face creased with the burden of his long-held secret. "Siki, I could not. I could not bring shame to his wife. To his children."

"Shame?" I asked, fearful of the answer he might give, but unable to stop the questions tumbling from my mouth. "Why would there be shame in his death? He died a warrior, did he not?"

"No, Siki, he did not." The old man clutched my hand, his clawed fingers digging deep in my palm. "Siki... I would not tell you this, but it seems you burn to have knowledge of it. I see you will not rest until you know the truth." A shaking sigh rattled his chest and tears began to trickle from his ancient eyes. "I found many bodies grouped together – slain by a Mexican ambush. Your father's was not amongst them. His was a great distance apart. Alone. He had fled from the fight. Deserted his brothers. Siki, my child ... your father died the death of a coward."

The horses of our tribe were roped with litters carrying tepees and hides, but we had brought many more animals from Mexico, and thus when we parted from our brothers and began our journey towards our Black Mountain home, I rode the dark mare of which I was so fond.

My people moved freely across the great land made by Ussen, the children playing and laughing, the women chattering and scolding, the men telling tales of hunting and battle. It was a journey of some days, and as we travelled I kept to myself, for I had much to brood upon. In doing so, I fell behind, and as we approached the uplands I found myself riding alone.

The old man had wearied himself in talking with me. Saying only "We will speak more of this. But not today," he had entered his tepee and dropped its flap against me. Though I had sought him before we went from the plateau, he had been sleeping. I had not bade him farewell and I could not help but think I would not see him again on the living earth.

The certainty of my father's death should have brought some relief to my troubled mind. And yet now I knew he had fled – abandoning his brothers to their deaths – and thus died a coward, and a traitor to his tribe. Punte had seen him run, I was certain, and had told his son – for how else could Keste have taunted me? But Chee remained in ignorance, so I must believe that his father had seen nothing. Golahka too had said naught. A new fear now draped itself around my neck, for I had seen Punte's look of fury. Would he keep silent now I was following the warrior's path? Or would whispers spread from ear to ear? How was I to endure if all the tribe knew of my father's disgrace?

Each Apache is answerable for none but himself. His own actions alone have the power to defame him. If a parent is dishonoured – even if he is banished from the tribe – no blemish falls upon his offspring. Each child starts his life afresh; a stain does not spread from one generation to the next and soil the innocent along with the guilty. This I knew. And yet I felt shame, sharp in my breast and as cold as the head of Tazhi's spear.

As I rode, my woman's curiosity could not leave alone the thought of my father, but nagged and tore at memories of him.

He had often swung me upon his shoulders and carried me between the tepees, exchanging an easy word here, a friendly greeting there. To me, it had seemed he was adored by all and I had taken a child's pride in his being so beloved. But now I was grown to womanhood, I wondered at it. For I knew well that unspoken enmities – untold divisions – may lie between adults that a child's eyes do not see. Courageous as my father had always seemed, I could not have known the truth of what lay in his heart.

When I crossed the plain, I was riddled with confusion. I doubted my father, I doubted myself, and I began to doubt my Power. So certain had I been that I could call my father from the afterlife. So certain had I been that because he did not come he must yet live. It seemed my Power was a weak and fractured thing.

Ahead of me, the last of my tribe rode the winding

path into the mountains. They were gone from my sight when the dark mare's hooves struck the rocky trail of our home range. I was in my own land, entering the high mountains where no Mexican had ever ventured. I rode incautious, my mind full, my attention elsewhere. Though I was in sun, my arms prickled with a sudden chill, and yet so deep in thought was I that I paid no heed. I had forgotten every lesson that Golahka had taught me.

It should not have taken the soft twang of a bowstring to remind me I had an enemy. One, moreover, who knew these mountains as well as I. One as skilled in hunting and tracking as the finest of our warriors, and whose aim surpassed all.

Yet it was not until an arrow pierced my thigh, pinning it to the dark mare's flank, that I remembered Keste.

The mare stumbled as the arrow struck, and I felt her hindquarters bunch for flight. But before she could run, a second arrow pierced her throat and she fell, trembling, to the ground. I felt her spirit slip from her as she rolled upon her side, her great weight trapping my other leg under her body. The bone of my shin snapped against the rock.

I lay unmoving, helpless as an infant strapped to its cradleboard, and waited for my death. But sending me swiftly to the afterlife was not Keste's intention. As I lay and no end came, I understood his mind. The mountain lion will not always kill its prey outright. Sometimes it will toy with it idly, for amusement, and thus it was with Keste. He did not wish me dead. Not yet. First he wished me pain.

I knew he would be coming down from the rocks where he had concealed himself. As in our fight with stones and slings, he wished to stand above me and see me quail before him. Now how grievously I felt the loss of my quiver of arrows. Tazhi's spear was cracked and broken in my fall. My only weapon was my flint-bladed knife, and trapped as I was, it was of little use against my enemy. And yet I needed something in my hand to defend myself from his cruelty. Dizzied with pain, I reached for my knife, and as I did so my hand brushed the pouch of ammunition that Golahka had given me.

The gun. It was slung across my back. I knew not how to use it. But Keste did not know that. And a gun is not silent. The glinting metal gave me hope.

When Keste came into view he was not watching me, but rather eyeing the trail to ensure no warriors had turned back to find me.

Hard indeed was it to wrestle the gun from my back. Blood streamed from my pinioned leg, and I was becoming weak. Yet I did so, struggling to feed it with a shot, and ramming it home as the Mexican had done. Twisting my body, I concealed the weapon until I could make use of it. I laid my head upon the ground, with a desperate wish that I would not sink into unconsciousness.

It was then that Keste came to me. His shadow was upon me, blotting out the sun, and I felt the chill of his hatred. I lay bleeding, broken, defenceless. I had to make him think I had lost all hope.

"Keste…" I whispered pleadingly, as my fingers fumbled for the gun's trigger. "I beg you…"

"You sought to take my place amongst the warriors," he said, his voice soft as the hiss of a serpent. "You! A girl whose father was traitor to his tribe! Now know that I have bested you."

He raised his bow again and aimed.

But Keste too had been slow to learn from the errors of the past. Once more he was deceived by me.

With my remaining strength, I pulled the gun from beneath me and fired.

I had no time to aim, and in truth I would scarce have known how to. The noise was what I desired, for it would alert our warriors to danger. They would come, and come swiftly. Keste knew it, and would have killed me before they arrived, had I not chanced to strike him. It was not a direct hit; I had but wounded him slightly. It seemed the shot had rebounded off the rock and a small splinter had pierced his bow arm. He bled. Clutching his wound lest falling drops make his trail easy to follow, Keste fled, melting into the rocks like grease in the fire.

It was not long before the softly moccasined feet of Golahka ran swiftly towards me. Kneeling beside me, he asked urgently, "Siki! Little sister... Speak! Do you live?"

I lived, but barely. The medicine man made many chants over me, and dressed my wounds with herbs that Ussen placed upon our land, but of this I knew nothing. It was not only the injuries to my legs that rendered me insensible – in firing my gun so poorly I had been hit by its recoil. The weapon had cracked against my skull, splitting the skin and driving me into darkness. I was carried to our camp on the back of Golahka, and now Hosidah – who could not tend Dahtet – cared for me with great skill, as lovingly as if I were her daughter.

In the days and nights that followed, I felt my own mother lingering at the doorway to the after-life, as though she waited to take my hand and welcome me into the Happy Place. It was a sore temptation to cease my struggle, to step willingly into her fond embrace, and leave hatred and enmity far behind.

But on the fourth night that followed Keste's ambush I heard someone call my name.

"Siki!"

Four times.

And then the voice of Ussen whispered in my ear.

"You will not die here, Siki, and you will not die now. You will live to be a warrior. Your people have need of you."

And with those words Ussen unrolled a vision before me. A vision whose meaning I did not comprehend, but which filled me with wondering awe. The red and black animals painted upon the tepee wall danced in the firelight; I watched them leap and spin. And then they gathered together as they had once before into the shape of a child – an infant whose skin was pale as the waxing moon. This time the image did not dissolve, but grew and spread in its intensity.

The child wept. It sat alone and helpless in the dust, its face pinched with hunger. There came a woman – an Apache – who fed the child with strips of meat from her pouch. She gave freely, for all will give of their best to strangers who come upon our land – this is the rule of hospitality – and besides, who could not aid a child?

The babe ate greedily, but was not satisfied. It begged for more, more, more, its cries rising to

163

hideous, demanding shrieks of command. No matter how quickly the woman fed the infant, she could not quell its hunger. And now it began to grow and swell until it stood tall as a pine. This monstrous infant stamped its foot until the ground beneath it shook.

Casting its eyes about our land, the child's gaze at last settled on the distant hills. There amongst the trees stood a dark-haired man. One hand shaded his eyes from the sun so that his face was obscured. He beckoned and the child walked towards the mountains.

The mountains of our home.

The vision's meaning was beyond my fevered comprehension. Sorely troubled, I fell into an uneasy, restless sleep.

It was fortunate that Keste had wished to maim before he killed me, for the arrow he sent into my thigh was not tipped with the poison he might have used had he simply intended to deal death swiftly. Some Apache know how to brew poison of such intensity that with the merest scratch the victim will sicken and die in but a few heartbeats. I did not doubt that Keste was one of them. But my wound was clean, and the flesh began quickly to heal.

Bones take longer; they must be rested, bound,

immobile, until they begin to knit. It was with irritable temper that I sat idle, my shin outstretched, feeling the strong hardness of my legs wither away until the muscle was soft and the skin slack as an aged man's. My hands I kept occupied shaping flint arrowheads until my quiver bristled with them: I would not be caught weaponless again. It was not so easy to fill my mind, and my thoughts returned always to Keste.

He had been trailed but had not been found. Of course he had not. Nor would he be, for Keste knew and excelled in every skill the Apache possess. He would keep himself hidden until he wished to strike once more. And now another certainty settled in my mind: Keste was the dark-haired man I had seen in the tent of the White Eyes. He had followed us from there with great swiftness, and could with equal speed have returned to them. And they would, by now, have moved on. In this great land, how could any even begin to seek him?

A new stricture descended upon our tribe in the days that followed, for if Keste had – as it seemed – tipped from haughty pride into madness, it was not I alone who was now his enemy. Any who had thwarted him must watch for their safety. Golahka was ever alert, ever wary, and Chodini moved with caution. Those boys who wished to begin training to become a warrior would have to wait; they could not go and test themselves for worthiness, for our chief would not permit any to go alone into the mountains.

The mother and father of Keste, and his young brother, moved around our camp with their heads down, their eyes fixed to the ground. They seemed like ones shamed by the actions of their son, and yet I could not be sure if it was so. For I had seen Punte's heart and knew of his anger. Thus I kept far from their tepee.

Dahtet's parents avoided them likewise. Her father trembled with rage when he considered how Keste had disgraced his child; the two men could not pass by each other without furious looks and muttered words. Her mother seemed to feel no wrath, but only fear: fear that gnawed at her in the darkness of the tepee; fear for her daughter. For when Keste had been hunted in the mountains, our warriors had found not a trace of Dahtet.

My broken leg was bound with sticks so that it might heal straight. After one moon, and with the aid of Golahka, I was able to move about the camp. As I sat propped on a rock, he began to teach me mastery of the gun. I disliked the weapon's great noise – with each shot it declared my whereabouts.

How could one be stealthy armed thus? And yet I had to admit its usefulness, for though it had knocked me senseless, it had also saved my life.

With the passage of two moons, I removed the splints from my leg and began to walk once more alone. At the start, I felt unsteady; the bone was mended, but my leg was wasted and my gait rolling and uneven.

In healing, I had grown soft and weak. I could not remain so. And thus with Chee and Ishta and Huten I resumed the training of the novice. Three more times I had to accompany the warriors before I could join their council. Before then, I needed to submit once more to Golahka's teaching.

"To live is to struggle," Golahka told us. "Each fight you have – even those you lose – will make you stronger for the next. Suffer. Struggle. Be strengthened."

We were to run to the mountain top as before, carrying water in our mouths that we would spit at Golahka's feet on our return.

On the first morning, when we ran the trail before sunrise, my lungs felt as though they would burst, my heart as if it would explode from my chest with the strain of keeping pace with my fellows. Even Huten outran me. I – who had once

167

been fleetest of foot and had caught a fleeing deer. Now I limped, ungainly as a hobbled horse. My body was sheened with heavy sweat, but I kept running until at last my leg was seized with such a powerful spasm that I tumbled headlong upon the path.

In the grey light, I found that Huten, Chee and Ishta had stopped with me. To my great surprise I saw that they kept me surrounded within their protecting circle as though they would stop Keste's arrows with their own bodies.

Chee spat out his water. "We do not leave you alone, Siki," he said. "For now, you see, we are all bound to you."

Since Tazhi had been slain, and indeed even while he walked the living earth, I had often felt the people of our tribe looked at me as one whose ways were different. I was so used to solitude that at first Chee's words alarmed me; I was nervous and felt some unease. But then – even as the rising sun drives the cold from the desert plain – I began to glow with sudden warmth. What pleasure was there in earning the respect – the friendship – of my brothers! I basked in the light of their esteem.

We returned from our run late. The sun had climbed into the sky as we descended, and Golahka was fast coming up the trail to find us. None of us could spit our water upon the ground before him – it had been lost when my leg's seizure halted our run.

Golahka was not interested in hearing our explanations. "Have you been gossiping as you dawdled upon the path?" he exclaimed. "This was not to be a maidens' outing! I thought you wished to be warriors? Acting thus, you shame yourselves. It must not happen again."

Loudly Golahka berated us, and yet to me there seemed little real temper in his voice. I had seen his expression when he viewed us ahead: the relief that we lived had been unmistakably etched upon his face.

It was many days until I could keep pace with Chee, and a whole moon had passed before I could outrun him as I had the previous summer. Much joy I felt when I pounded into the camp ahead of him, spat my mouthful of water at Golahka's feet and saw my triumph reflected in the warrior's black eyes.

My former strength had returned, but when Chodini led a small number of men to hunt deer on the broad plain, I did not go with them. For my chief had drawn me aside, and said, "Siki. Daughter, I know well you are a fine hunter. And yet I would ask you to remain amongst the women. Keste will not look for you there, as he may watch those who hunt."

I yielded to his wisdom, and yet it was with simmering resentment against Keste that I went to gather the nuts and berries that hung ripe upon the trees. My clumsy fingers seemed to squash as many as I saved. The tedium of the task left my mind free to wander, and again and again it returned to the memories of my father. I picked them over, looking for signs of rottenness, even as I did with the plucked berries.

I recalled the time – at six summers old – I had been mounted upon a small pony and recklessly challenged my father to a race.

"What will you give me if you lose?" he said.

So I had wagered the doll my mother had lovingly stitched for me. My doll against his flint-bladed knife.

We set off, and at once I knew the rashness of my gamble, for my father's horse took but one step to my pony's three. He could outride me with ease, and yet, teasingly, he kept just within reach. Hot, angry tears pricked my eyes and blurred my vision.

"Yield," he shouted over his shoulder.

I would not. I kept urging my pony forward. And in turning to torment me, my father did not see the rabbit hole that pierced the earth before him. His mount missed its step, stumbled and he fell.

I bested him. I kept my doll. His knife was the one I still carried at my waist.

There had been much laughter from those who had watched our race, and my father had joined in the merriment, lifting me off my pony's back and swinging me through the air, before setting me high upon his shoulders. But there had been an achingly long pause before he did so – a long, breathless silence when his eyes had met mine. I saw he was enraged. He could not endure losing.

I crushed a berry between my fingers and smeared its juice into my palm, as I considered that in this, my father was like Keste.

As a girl, I had seen only perfection. Yet now I looked afresh with warrior's eyes, and began to see the faults that tarnished him. They were tiny fissures like those in a clay vessel. But the slightest crack will split a pot apart when it is heated. Had it been thus with my father?

I said little during those long days of gathering, but listened instead to the gossip of the women. Huten was with us, not standing guard, but deftly picking as he chattered. With each step the rest of the novices had taken along the warrior's path, Huten had seemed to fall further behind. It caused him much anguish. Yet here he was all peaceful content. I watched him, thinking how strange was

171

our destiny. For had I possessed half his skill in the women's tasks, I would have stayed amongst them, and not ventured to be a warrior. I would never have provoked the enmity of Keste, and the fate of my father would have lain, unquestioned, in the shadows where it belonged.

I knew I should leave it there, look no more upon it. I pushed thoughts of my concerns far away, and let Huten's laughter fill my ears and flood my mind. Warriors had come with us, and stood alert and watchful as we worked, but of Keste there was no sign. Untroubled, undisturbed, we returned to our tepees some days later, baskets brimming with food.

It was not so for Chodini.

After an absence of seven sunrises, he came back to our camp empty-handed. The men had tracked through the northern hills and far across the wide plain but had not been able to find any herd of deer that grazed there.

Instead they had come upon a settlement of White Eyes. Many soldiers, who had hacked down living trees, and gouged rocks from the earth, and had fashioned for themselves a large dwelling in the great land Ussen had created for the Apache.

Chodini related his tale with no sense of alarm. He was troubled by the lack of game, for without meat his tribe faced hunger, but the coming of the White Eyes concerned him less. Our land was broad and spacious; there was room for all to walk upon it. He had greeted the strangers and had bid them welcome. He had sworn brotherhood.

I did not know the cause of my unease. I did not link my disquiet to the vision of the child Ussen had sent me, for what bond could there be between that monstrous infant and this regiment of soldiers? I said nothing. The hunt's failure was of greater importance. Chodini would soon ride to the east of our mountains, where he would once again seek deer.

Many of our tribe had come forth when Chodini returned, and now stood anxious, for it had been near eighteen moons since Tazhi had died, and winter would soon be upon us once more. The tribe was not well provisioned with food. Thus Golahka spoke to all when he said, "I will go into Mexico for cattle. I depart at sunrise. Will any ride with me?" His eyes burned at the prospect of a return into the land of his enemy.

It was not a war party that Golahka sought. For stealth, the numbers he chose would be few. Yet none but Golahka had an appetite to return so soon into Mexico. The memory of our losses there was fresh in many minds, the grief still raw. Such a journey would be fraught with danger, and many chose instead to fill their families' bellies in hunting deer, or antelope, or rabbits in the upland meadows. For some time, none spoke.

Then a voice broke the stillness. "I will come." It was Naite, nephew to Chodini, who had but lately become a warrior. His desire to prove himself was strong, but he was also of sound judgement and even temper.

Clasping Naite's shoulder, Golahka said, "I am glad of it. You will ride well."

When the next man spoke, a murmur rippled amongst the watchers, for it was Punte, father of Keste, his eyes downcast as if expecting to be refused. "I too will follow you into Mexico."

Golahka gave a swift nod. "You are welcome, brother," he said, though for an instant I saw a flicker of doubt in his eyes. Punte had disowned his son when Keste made himself outcast. But the bonds of blood run deep. Keste had made Golahka his enemy: would his father do the same?

No other warrior spoke, and the tribe went back to its tasks. I turned to go, for I knew that so few warriors would scarce have need of a novice. But Golahka called my name, and was suddenly before me, eyes glinting blackly, saying, "Siki, you have not spoken. Do you wish to come?"

I was startled to be asked; if I went it would be my second journey and thus my second step along the warrior's path. I was young to be advancing so fast, and was astounded to be honoured so far above my fellows. My mouth did not at once obey the command of my mind. When my voice at last burst forth from my gaping lips it resounded like the crack of a gun. "Yes! Yes ... indeed."

"Then it shall be so. Make your preparations."

A raid does not have the sacred solemnity of a war party, although as a novice the strictures I had to observe were the same. But there were no dances in the firelight on the eve of our departure, no dawn farewells from the assembled tribe. Instead, at sunrise we silently slipped away towards the south.

For speed we rode. When we neared the land of our enemy, the horses would be hobbled and concealed, that we might proceed on foot for secrecy.

We moved with great caution, even upon our own land, for neither Golahka nor I knew if the eyes of Keste followed us. And yet as we went forth, I felt my spirit rise with the joy of freedom, for in truth the friendly solicitude of my fellows had begun to weary me. I had scarce been able to move without Chee or Ishta or Huten by my side – they had become as shadows to me. Grateful as I was, I could not help but feel oppressed to be watched so constantly.

And yet as we journeyed, I found I had but changed their vigilance for another's. The eyes of Punte – their expression carefully veiled – seemed always to be upon me. As we rode, as we rested, as I tended the horses, gathered wood, cooked, I felt the weight of his gaze. Perhaps he thought to find me wanting. If so, I was determined to give him no cause to complain. I worked hard; I left no task undone. And yet still those eyes followed me. Punte had seen my father flee. I began to think he looked for signs of cowardice in me, fearing I too might betray my fellows.

A strange party we made, full of unease and mistrust. Punte watched me, and Golahka watched Punte. Naite alone seemed untroubled by the currents that flowed silent between us. I wondered what would be the outcome of this raid, for warriors must fight alongside those they trust. Dislike may exist, as long as there is also respect. There seemed to be naught but suspicion between Golahka and Punte, and I hoped it would not bring with it ill luck.

For two days we rode, entering the western edges of the Chokenne range on the third sunrise. Golahka had thought to cross the plain and follow the twisting river into Mexico. But we were surprised to see the smoke of fires below us. Pines had been hacked from the hillside, leaving the once wooded slope naked and exposed, raw stumps bleeding sap. And when I looked down at the plain I started, for it seemed to be covered by a dark stain. As I watched, I saw it was a settlement of many soldiers; it was their clothing that appeared to colour the land. Many White Eyes were making another huge dwelling; these were not those whom Chodini had encountered in the north of our own range. I marvelled at the number of these strangers and wondered from where they had come. Even as we watched they drove metal stakes along a felled tree's length until its body was split in two. Could they not hear the tree spirits crying in their distress?

The habit of caution flowed in Golahka's blood, and thus, frowning with displeasure at their intrusion, he changed our direction to avoid meeting the White Eyes.

In two more days, he took us into a different part of Mexico – one where I had never yet travelled.

And yet I knew it. The curve of the hill. The shape of the distant mountain. The formation of the rock. I knew it so well that it stopped me upon my horse. The land held me still. I recognized this place: Ussen had drawn its image upon the dark river waters of Jujio.

I had seen it from the doorway of a Mexican dwelling. Looked upon it as the child was taken by an Apache warrior. Up that hill had the Chokenne ridden. My eyes slid down to the grass; there I could discern the faint line of an adobe wall that had crumbled to nothing. My horse's hooves were planted where the woman's blood had spilt upon the beaten earth floor. Here she had died.

And as I stared, trembling, at the grass that now grew there, it blurred, and upon it Ussen drew another vision.

I saw many Black Mountain warriors on horseback. I knew these men. Ozheh, son of Chodini, came first. Beside him rode Golahka, looking as he had when he had newly joined our tribe – before the slaughter of Tehineh had carved grim lines across his face. Torrez came, with Punte and Chee's father, Biketsin. Jotah, and Potro and Hozhen – all now dead – passed me. They rode on, without a pause. And now came my father. Ashteh the warrior. Bold. Fearless. Handsome. I saw him clearly.

His horse stopped suddenly, as mine had done. He looked about him with shock. His mouth fell open. His brows furrowed.

As he sat frozen upon his horse, Ozheh came to him. My father roused himself, masking his expression at once. I heard not his words, but I saw

Ozheh's gestures telling my father to go ahead with Potro in advance of the rest of the warriors, for my father's skill as a scout had been great. Leaving their horses, the scouts went swiftly forward on foot. I watched my father until he vanished from view.

So lost was I in what I saw that I was not aware Golahka had ridden back to where I had stopped. Only when he reached from his horse and put his hand upon my shoulder did I jerk back to the living earth.

When he asked, "You have seen something, little sister?" I could do naught but answer, "My father. My father passed this way."

Golahka spoke gently. "He did. We are near to the place where we were ambushed. I see it gives you unease. You are like a horse that smells blood. Come, Siki, we will go by a different way."

Without another word, Golahka changed our direction once more, and we rode far from that place, Punte's eyes heavy upon me. Distance brought no relief. I felt the weight of my father's amulet in my pouch and rued that I had not destroyed it as is the custom of my people. With each hoof beat the turquoise beads banged at my hip, searing me with the knowledge of my father's disgrace.

I knew of his treachery, and yet even now Ussen sought to show me more. With each fragment, each snatch of truth, the shame I felt burned more hotly. How much more could I endure before I – like the sage leaf – would crumble to ashes?

We rode in search of cattle, mules, horses – anything that would feed our people and keep them from starvation in the coming winter. We moved stealthily and did not attract attention by making attacks upon our enemies. But well I knew that if we were once seen, the Mexican would fire upon us without hesitation. Without mercy.

We hobbled our horses in a valley through which a stream ran and where sweet grass grew for them to feed upon, and set forth on foot. But we had scarce touched the soil of Mexico when my palms began to prick.

To Golahka I spoke the words that Ussen placed in my mouth.

"To the west. Two Mexicans ... a wagon ... mules."

"How far?" he asked.

"They are very close."

"Then we have not much time."

He swiftly scanned the landscape. We were on the side of a steeply sloping hill. At its foot ran the path the wagon would take. No cover was close by it, and thus we remained high above, placing ourselves behind such rocks and bushes as would give us concealment. We held still, and waited.

The rising cloud of dust thrown up by the wagon's wheels came closer, and soon they were below us. There were indeed two men, sitting upon a cart drawn by a single horse. Behind it, roped together in a long line, were many mules – all heavily laden. The men were not soldiers, but farmers. Suddenly my heart misgave me, and I regretted that I had drawn Golahka's attention to them. For had I not once seen into the mind of my enemy and felt pity? I did so now. I did not wish these men to die.

"Enough meat to feed the whole tribe," whispered Golahka, pulling back his bowstring.

He fired at the driver, but at the very instant his arrow flew forth, the man bent to brush a fly from his boot. It missed its mark, and thudded harmlessly into the wooden seat between the two men. A breath of relief escaped from me – a sound that made Golahka's eyes narrow with displeasure. He cursed, for now these men knew of our presence and would surely defend themselves. As he reached for another arrow, Naite and Punte descended the hill to stop the Mexicans fleeing before the mules were lost to us.

But the actions of these men were so surprising that Naite and Punte halted, frozen in their tracks, and Golahka never released his second arrow. They did not attempt to fight, nor did they whip their horse into flight. Instead, with high-pitched screams, they abandoned everything, jumping from their cart and running away along the track as fast as a pair of stampeding donkeys.

So startled by this was Golahka that he let them flee. He looked at me, eyebrows raised, his jaw hanging open. And then his loud laugh rang out amongst the rocks and set them shaking.

"You bring me good fortune, little sister," he said, smiling. "Never have provisions been won so easily!"

My heart joyed in his delight, and I was greatly relieved that he seemed so quickly to forget my treacherous gasp of relief. I was determined that I would not show such weakness again.

Coming down from the hill, we at once set about freeing the horse from its harness, for we had no need of the cart. Without examining the goods the mules were laden with, we led them away from that place, towards where our horses were hobbled, for although the men had fled, Mexican troops were a constant danger. There we split the mule train in two. Punte and Naite took half the animals in one direction; Golahka and I followed a different route. Until we arrived back at our mountain home we knew well that pursuit might come at any time. With so many animals we would be easy to track, and thus we had to move swiftly.

Before we parted, Punte looked at me. I did not know if he had heard my gasp, but he gave a small nod as though the question that troubled him had been answered. But whether it was for good or ill, I knew not.

As Golahka and I returned, constantly we were alert. Constantly we were cautious. Yet no pursuit came, and we met no dangers. We rode laughing into our camp, to the great joy of our people; though Chodini had hunted long and far, game had been scarce indeed.

Only when we were safe amongst the tepees did we unload the mules, and what they carried caused us great puzzlement. There were several hundred waxen balls of a strong-smelling yellow substance that we took to be a foodstuff. We knew not what to call it, nor how to eat it.

Punte had been captured by Mexicans as a boy and had spent three long summers as a slave on an estancia before he escaped and returned to his people. He knew their ways. Examining the booty, he declared it to be cheese.

Thus we survived that long cold winter: feasting daily on mule meat and cheese. It was good to have full bellies. But in truth, as the sweet spring air began to warm the mountains, we had long had our fill of it.

* * *

Cheese was not the only new foodstuff we encountered that winter. Chodini and many other warriors made journeys to Fort Andrews, the dwelling the White Eyes had fashioned in the north of our range, to trade for provisions.

It was not trade alone that drew the warriors forth – there was a great curiosity about these men and their unfamiliar ways. On one occasion, Ozheh came back with a sack of flour, and none knew what it was, nor what to do with it. We gathered round, sniffing, dipping fingers in and tasting the strange powder. Once more Punte explained its purpose.

"It is a pounded grain," he pronounced. "It must be mixed with water and shaped into a long cake."

The wife of Ozheh took it away and spent much time puzzling over its best use. Later, her hair sheened with a fine layer of dust, her fingers stuck together with a thick white paste, she presented Ozheh with an odd, misshapen cake. He chewed long and hard, and all watched his expression with breathless interest.

For a while, his face gave nothing away, but then he suddenly spat upon the ground, and ejected the lump without attempting to swallow.

"Foul as a long-dead toad!" he exclaimed, and the crowd burst into noisy laughter. "How can the

White Eyes eat such things? Small wonder they are so pale and soft! This is not the food of men!"

To the teasing shouts of his fellows, Ozheh loaded the sack once more onto his horse and began the long ride back to the settlement of the White Eyes. He had given one good blanket for the value-less powder; he would demand its return.

Ozheh's cake caused many smiles and much amusement. But not all the White Eyes' provisions were so unpalatable.

It was with the White Eyes that Chodini first tasted coffee, returning to our camp his horse laden with sacks of a bitter green bean. Roasted and ground they became appetizing, and soon our whole tribe had developed a passion for the strong-smelling liquid. The women were kept busy twining and coiling baskets to exchange for coffee and sugar with which to sweeten it. Our men also bartered for the White Eyes' fiery liquor, and would then drink until the supply they had gained was exhausted. Many a warrior would come back from the fort and soon be found lying insensible in his tepee, to wake the next morning with a sorely aching head.

Friendship flowed between our peoples, and I wondered at my own reluctance to make contact with these strangers. Their presence gave me great unease, and each time our warriors rode towards their dwelling my mind was filled with foreboding. And yet it came to nothing. Each time, they returned safe. I began to doubt my own judgement. These men were guests on our land. Why should I dread them?

And thus – as the leaves' buds began to swell – I dismissed my misgivings as the fanciful imaginings of a novice, and when Chodini next rode north to the White Eyes, I went with him.

In my mind, I had imagined the White Eyes' dwelling to be as that of the Mexican. Ours is a dry country, and those who make buildings often fashion them from earth bricks, baked in the sun. I had expected to see small adobe houses, grouped together. I was unprepared for the high walls that suddenly rose – sheer as the rock face – from the plain before me, and my eyes grew wide with surprise. It seemed that these White Eyes wished to shut out the wide sky and the sweet grass as though they were things to fear – to be kept at bay. I wondered that they chose to remain upon our land when such terror of it was in their hearts.

Many men watched as we approached. All were armed with rifles, belts of bullets slung about their waists. Panic rose within me, yet I knew not why.

Chodini smiled and called a greeting, and our party of ten warriors was welcomed inside Fort Andrews.

The White Eyes' chief came forth to greet Chodini, embracing him as a brother. My stomach lurched with disgust, for his face was disfigured by an unnatural growth of hair. The Apache are smooth-cheeked, and even in great age their hair grows thick and strong upon their heads. When this man removed his hat, I saw his hair had slid from the top of his head and come to rest upon his chin. The skin of his crown was smooth as an egg, and as hotly red as if it had been heated in a fire.

This hair-faced chief called for coffee and, sitting, he and Chodini drank it side by side, talking slowly in the Spanish tongue they shared. We traded such goods as we had brought for ammunition, coffee and sugar. All was well.

And yet I was like a dog whose hackles are raised no matter how many soothing words are spoken, and whose low growl refuses to die in its throat. From somewhere – I could not determine where – came a chill that caused my arms to bump like the flesh of a plucked bird. As I looked about me at these men, I felt that their eyes – even as they smiled – concealed contempt, as if they thought themselves superior to those whose land they walked upon. Though the White Eyes' chief clasped hands with

Chodini and swore friendship, I sensed an enmity lurking beneath the surface. It would take the smallest of scratches to bring it forth.

Seemingly, that scratch was Keste.

One moon after Chodini and I had returned from the White Eyes' settlement, the yucca stretched forth its green shoots and the women went to harvest them. At Chodini's request I went with them, not to harvest, but to give protection, for upon the flat desert plain there was little cover should an enemy approach.

Chodini rode alone to hunt the antelope. He met with success, and was returning with a fine doe tied to the saddle of his horse. In great thirst, he stopped at the spring near Fort Andrews.

New buildings had been fashioned either side of the rock from which the water gushed forth, and here a group of twelve or so soldiers had gathered. Chodini at once smelt the strong liquor on their breath and was wary. Full well he felt the subtle threat of their presence. But his horse had hunted long and hard, and needed to be watered. Chodini approached.

Greeting them, our chief asked the men what they did there, and they told him they had been sent to defend the spring. At this Chodini could do naught but laugh, thinking they spoke in jest. "From what?" he asked them. "From whom do you give it protection? You think the water might be slain, or captured?"

Chodini's horse lowered its head to drink and Chodini bent and filled his water vessel. When he stood once more, he found his path blocked by a brash young man who wore stripes – pointed like arrows – upon the arm of his dark coat.

In a tone of barely concealed contempt, the man began to speak. It seemed that one of their number had lately been slain by the arrows of an Apache. Chodini had no cause to doubt him, yet he wondered at the man's rudeness, for our chief had ever been courteous to the White Eyes. Carefully he explained that the deed was none of his doing: all the warriors of our tribe were bound by Chodini's vow of brotherhood. It might perhaps be an act of Keste's, he said, for Keste alone was beyond the jurisdiction of his chief.

"If this is so," he added, "and he has returned to these mountains, we also have much to fear. He is no friend to my tribe. We thought him in the south. I must give my people warning."

Chodini made to mount his horse, but found himself halted by the soldier, who now grasped his arm.

"You lie," he said. "And we will have compensation. The doe will be payment for it. And your horse too."

Chodini was rendered speechless with outrage. Not believe the word of a warrior? Not believe the word of a chief? The insult to his honour incensed him.

And yet it grew worse. Much worse. Encouraged by Chodini's silence, the soldier began to swagger.

"We should take this redskin to the fort," he told his men. "There he will face justice." He tried to lay hands upon Chodini and force him along with them. But the men were drunk, and our chief was not.

Of necessity, Chodini abandoned both the doe and his fine warhorse. By dodging, running, creeping and freezing upon his knees did Chodini, greatest of chiefs, leader of the Black Mountain Apache, return to his tribe.

Humiliated.

Dishonoured.

Hungry for revenge.

Events came hard upon us that spring, one following another as closely as a line of roped mules.

While Chodini sat brooding – for such an outrage was not to be endured – Sotchez, chief of the Chokenne Apache, entered the mountains of our home, bringing news that pierced us with fresh anguish.

The women and children of his tribe had gone out to gather shoots of the yucca even as ours had done. But the Chokenne women had not returned. When the warriors went forth to seek them, they found stripling boys – young novices – who had tried to defend their mothers slain upon the earth. The rest had been taken.

"You tracked them?" It was Golahka who spoke.

"We did. They were taken to Marispe, to the mine. There they are enslaved by the Mexicans."

"Goyenne?" His daughter's name was wrung from the throat of Chodini.

Sotchez nodded. "Our son also. This is why I come."

Chodini had already begun to gather his weapons. Sotchez needed not to ask for help. No warrior council was there. Word spread fast throughout the camp, and those who chose the warpath readied themselves at once. Speed was everything. All knew that when the Mexican stole women and children as slaves they might be carried far into the heart of Mexico where none would find them. But these Chokenne were yet close to the border; they might perhaps be recovered before they were taken further. Many warriors would be needed to free them; the gold mines of the

Mexican were known to have troops crawling over them as numerous as the fleas on a dog.

All was confusion in the camp. Chodini selected those men who would stay, for well he knew our own women and children must be protected. Amongst them was Chee, who glowed with pride to be entrusted with such a task. Bidding him a swift farewell, I took my weapons, and prepared myself for the journey ahead. Thus I would take my third step along the warrior's path.

Strange it seemed to enter the Chokenne camp, for it was near empty. No children played; no women chattered. But one fire burned, and around it were grouped the grim faces of warriors readied for battle.

We sat in a circle upon the ground, Sotchez at the centre. It was Sotchez whose family had been taken, Sotchez whose tribe's heart had been torn from it, and thus Sotchez would direct the battle. In the clear night air, he began to describe the place his people had been taken to.

"There is a narrow canyon two days' journey from here. At its head lies the entrance to the mine. There are many soldiers to defend it, positioned high amongst the rocks. My brothers, this will not be an easy fight. I must warn you our losses will be many." He paused awhile, letting his words sink into the silence. It is not the Apache way to fight when heavy losses are certain, and Sotchez knew how great a favour was the one he asked. "I do not force any to come."

"You do not," murmured Chodini. "This fight is ours too."

As Sotchez spoke of his battle plans, I ceased to hear him. While I sat staring into the fire, shapes began to form in the flames. Women and children, laden heavily as mules, shuffled wearily over a rope bridge that spanned a swollen river. Suddenly they stopped and stared wildly about them, as though afraid. Apache warriors swarmed into the canyon, and were fired upon by Mexicans. In the dancing flames I saw the proud face of Goyenne, and beside her Denzhone, wife of Pocito. Both reached for the hands of their children, their faces torn with terror. A Mexican sword was raised high, and cut the ropes that held the bridge. It fell. The women and children of the Chokenne dropped into the torrent, weighted by the burdens strapped upon their backs, and sank under the water like a handful of stones.

The words fell from my mouth before I knew it. "They will perish."

All eyes turned coldly to me. For a novice to speak was an offence; to interrupt a chief was an insult past imagining. None knew how to fill the silence that fell, until at last Sotchez spat angrily, "Better they should perish than live as slaves."

A loud rumble of agreement ran through the warriors. To the free Apache imprisonment is agony: the cruellest torture the Mexican can devise. Before the murmurs died down, I realized that Golahka was speaking softly into the ear of the Chokenne chief. From the movement of his head, I knew he talked of me.

And thus, when Sotchez spoke again, it was to ask, "You have seen this, sister?"

I nodded.

"Did Ussen show you more?"

I nodded again. After the women and children had dropped into the river, I had seen the image of a man burning brightly in the fire – a man nailed through hands and feet upon crossed branches. It was the effigy I had found long ago in the deserted dwelling, but I knew not why I should see it now.

Slowly – my face hot, my mouth clumsy with awkwardness at speaking before the assembled warriors – I described my vision. I did not know its meaning. No one did. Until at last Punte spoke. "The tortured man is their god."

Their god? I was astonished at the Mexican's savagery, for who would drive nails through a god's hands until he screamed in agony? What manner of man would then fashion the image of this horror that he might look upon it daily?

Punte continued thoughtfully, "On each seventh day, the Mexicans gather together in the house they call church to pay worship to this god."

"All of them?" Golahka's voice was sharp as though he had begun to detect meaning in this strangeness.

"So it was in the place I was enslaved."

"Then that is the time to strike." Golahka's black eyes flashed with triumph. "And perhaps thus we may free the captives without their loss."

It was agreed, then, that we would not travel as a massed body of warriors that would alarm the Mexicans and drive them to murder their slaves. Furtively we would set forth, a small band of scouts travelling ahead to observe the mine and determine the best moment to attack. The Apache neither name the days, nor number them, and it was only by covert observation that we would know which was the Mexicans' sacred day. Thereafter we must act as opportunity allowed. Runners would pass from the scouts to the main body of our force, and instruct them how to proceed.

Sotchez went with the scouts, as did Chodini, who, though he was an aged man, was still a lithe and powerful warrior. Goyenne was his daughter: even had he been crippled and bent, none would have refused his right to go first into battle. Golahka was also to go ahead, along with Pocito, and Punte, who knew the ways of the Mexican.

And so was I. Novice though I was, Golahka took me aside and spoke quietly. "We have need of you, Siki, if you will come. Ussen has shown you much, little sister. Perhaps he will speak again."

I agreed. Of course I agreed. I could do naught else.

We did not like to move at night, but for greater secrecy we did so. The moon was bright and lit our way, and we walked hoping that we would not lay our feet upon snakes and scorpions.

At dawn on the third day, we came upon the narrow canyon from above. We had rubbed earth into our skin and with dampened clay set grass into our hair; thus we would blend into the rocks and not be observed by the many guards we knew to be there. Keeping low, we crept towards the edge. A deep cleft beneath a jutting boulder, where trees overhung, was large enough to conceal us, and from there we could observe all that happened.

A torrent divided the valley floor, a rope bridge strung across it. On the side furthest from us was a narrow path leading towards a dark chasm that pierced the belly of the earth like an open wound. Below us were several houses – adobe dwellings one storey high. The largest stood at the narrow end of the valley. A bell hung from a tower above its door, and the crossed sticks made the sign of their tortured god.

Punte pointed at it. "That is their church," he whispered.

Sotchez answered, "Then that is where they shall die."

This valley was a loathsome place.

Gold is sacred to Ussen. In our mountain home small pieces can sometimes be found in the streams, and these we know as the tears of the sun. My father had once delighted in their colour, and kept many such pieces in the pouch at his waist. But in truth they were of little use for anything but ornament, for the metal is too soft to form an arrowhead. To pick up what lies upon the land is permitted, but Ussen forbids us to dig in search of gold. The earth is our mother; she feeds us with her bounty. How could any then hack into her living flesh?

To see these Mexicans carving into the body of Mother Earth was a sight that filled me with sick revulsion. Could they not hear her anguished cries?

Could they not feel the mountain spirits quaking with anger? Could they not taste the wrath of Ussen? No. Their ears were stoppered by greed; their hearts were in thrall to this yellow metal. They would deprive our people of their liberty in pursuit of more, more, more. And yet these Mexicans had made themselves captive too. They could not see the ropes that bound them, but their souls were enslaved. Their love of gold cost them their own freedom.

As we watched, the sun's rays began to lighten the canyon, and movements came from below. Filing out of a small, squat building were the women and children of the Chokenne. There were Goyenne and her son. There Denzhone, the wife of Pocito, one hand upon the shoulder of her son, the other clutching her small daughter. Their faces showed nothing. No one wept; no one cried; not even the smallest child let out a whimper. With the dignity and grace of the Apache, they stepped out of their prison. But even across this great distance I could feel the horror of their confinement. The very air stank of despair.

Our people were loaded with baskets upon their backs as if they were mules: brute, stubborn beasts with no sense and little feeling. Shouting harsh words of command, the Mexican guards waved their guns and forced the Chokenne to cross the rope bridge and enter the dark tunnel which split the earth.

There was a movement to my left, and instinctively I froze, pressed against the chasm where the scouts lay hidden. It was as well I did, for a Mexican guard paced the top of the canyon. He walked on without seeing me. It was then that I knew the full peril of the captives' imprisonment and saw the enormity of the task before us.

Any guard that stood at the top of the canyon could fire with ease upon those who entered below. Yet if a force came from above, those in the canyon would be alerted at once, and would slay the Chokenne in an instant. To divine when the Mexicans would enter the dwelling of their god was of vital importance. As Golahka had said, it was the only time an attack could succeed. And the warriors had to know when to move, for even if many of the Mexicans were contained within the building, still there would be guards outside to be overpowered, and overpowered simultaneously.

But how were we to discover the knowledge that we needed? The answer slipped into my mind as soon as the question was formed. *The women will know*. They had been held in this dread place for many sunrises: they would know the ways of their captors. Someone would have to enter the canyon unseen, and ask them.

Golahka, it seemed, had had the same thought,

for when I whispered the words into his ear he nodded without surprise. "At night," he answered. "It can only be done at night."

All that long day, we could do nothing but wait, looking down at the women and children who laboured as slaves for the cruel Mexicans. We watched them crossing and recrossing the bridge, laden so heavily with ore-filled rocks that their knees buckled beneath them. It was torment to Chodini to remain so, and for Sotchez, who itched to slit the throat of each guard that passed by where he lay. And were it not for Golahka's warning hand, fingers pressed so hard into the shoulder of Pocito that his nails drew forth blood, Pocito would have given himself and his fellow scouts away.

What caused him to flinch so was the sight of his wife and children coming once more across the rope bridge. As they neared the side below us, his son staggered beneath his burden and fell. The sound of what passed next rose clearly from the canyon. The boy spoke – a curse of exhausted despair expelled through his lips. But it was a word of Spanish.

"¡Demonios!"

At once the guard who had stood with his gun pointed towards the captives put aside his weapon and bent to aid the boy.

"*¿Hablas español?*" he asked urgently. "*¿Eres mexicano?*"

The boy shook his head frantically, reaching for his mother. But in understanding the guard's question he had betrayed himself. The guard ripped the boy's basket from his back, calling to his comrades. "*¡Mexicano! Este mocoso es mexicano!*"

No matter that the boy screamed for his mother. No matter that she wept and pleaded for his return. Roughly she was thrown aside, falling into the dust as the boy she loved as her own was carried, sobbing, fighting, away from her.

Small wonder that Pocito ached to help her. Much control it took him to restrain himself under the hand of Golahka and remain still. His body stiffened until it was rigid with effort, and he had then the look of Keste when the burning leaf had been placed on his arm. But this pain was far worse than any of the body. This was beyond enduring. It pierced us all as we watched from our hiding place.

For well we knew that now Pocito's son was taken he would be kept by the Mexicans and reclaimed as their own. On the seventh day he would be amongst those who entered the dwelling place of the suffering god.

And when he did so, Pocito's son would perish.

* * *

201

At nightfall the guard changed. Men came up from the canyon to replace those who had stalked the rocks through the long day, and they stood smoking and talking to one another. It was then that our group of scouts held a hasty council.

The moon cast shadows of the guards across the bare rocks of the canyon. The clear sky held no trace of cloud. To creep into the valley on such a night would be a task fraught with danger. And yet there was a fissure in the rocks that was in shadow, for the moon's beams could not light it. A jagged crack that ran like a lightning bolt from top to bottom: so thin it would admit but one small person to creep along it.

"I will go alone." I spoke swiftly, pointing to the fissure. "There! I will ask the women which is the seventh day."

"No," said Chodini. "You are too young for this task."

But Golahka shook his head, whispering, "She is small. Silent. We must let her go. Truly, my chief. Ussen walks beside her."

Thus it was decided, and as the fresh guards took their places for the night watch, I handed my gun and arrows to Golahka, for they would do naught but impede me. Only my flint knife I took with me, and this I tucked in the fold of my moccasin. The great warrior could make no sound that might alert the guards, so he spoke not, but from the clasp he gave my arm I drew much strength.

When the men below extinguished their fires and began to sleep, I started to move.

The first part of my journey was the most dangerous, for before I could reach the cleft I had to climb down a bare stone face where the moon was brightest and where – should any guard chance to look – I would be an easy target. Fingers and toes braced in cracks, it was a slow, precipitous climb. The guards did not look, and with great relief I slid into the cleft's tight embrace. Now I could breathe once more, and for a moment I stayed, forcing my heart to slow its rapid beat. Then I began to creep slowly down towards the valley floor.

For some length the descent was steady and I was able to slip noiselessly along the rough passage. I had gone, by my reckoning, one third of the way, when the pass became so narrow I thought I could not proceed. I reached forward, and guessed that the fissure opened out from this place for I could feel nothing beyond. I forced myself down, feet first, scraping the skin from my legs, expelling all breath as my torso grated against the harsh stone, and suddenly I was through. Not only through, but dropping into the blackness, and landing hard on a rocky shelf below. I would surely have been discovered had the sound of my fall not been covered by a commotion that then came from where the Chokenne were held captive.

Men – their voices made loud by liquor – had opened the door where the Chokenne were held and had pulled out a woman. It was Denzhone, who had stood beside the barred window, her small daughter on her hip, hoping to glimpse her son. They threw her daughter back inside, casting the child to the ground as if she were a creature with no feeling. And now – scarcely troubling to drag Denzhone into the shadows where they could not be seen – they began to force themselves upon her.

Bile rose within me, for such had been done to my mother before she was killed. But I must not vomit; I must make no sound. I tried to suck in lungfuls of air, but it seemed putrid with the stench of men's sweat. I bit upon my knuckles to stop the scream that swelled in my throat.

Cold hatred calmed me. I gathered my wits, drew a steady breath, and continued my descent. Rage quelled my horror. For this act, these Mexicans would perish. None – not one – would survive.

I reached the valley floor and fell at once to my knees, creeping and freezing in the pools of darkness towards the building which housed the captives. I would not approach it from the front for fear I would be seen. I could but hope that a window opened at the rear through which I could whisper to the women.

I was fortunate. There was a slit, smaller than a child's head. I peered through and saw their cell, illumined in patches by the moon. By the time I reached it, the men had finished with Denzhone and she sat, dry-eyed, on the earth floor, her back to the wall, her small daughter clinging around her neck. Corncobs had been scattered carelessly on the ground, as if the Chokenne were birds that peck in the dust for food. It remained uneaten, and I saw from the gaunt faces of the women, the hollow cheeks of the children, that they had chosen to escape their confinement through starvation.

Closest to the opening was Goyenne, her back stiff and proud even in this degradation. To her would I speak. But how could I attract her attention, without risking the notice of the guard who paced beyond the door?

Undoing the strip of cloth that bound my hair, I tied a pebble in the fold at one end, and this I poked through the slit. It made not a sound, but Goyenne's eye was drawn to the small movement, and I felt an answering tug upon the cloth.

"Sister," I whispered. "Help comes. But we must

know when to strike. On what day do the Mexicans enter the dwelling where they worship?"

Goyenne answered at once. "In two sunrises. All but the guards at the canyon's top will enter."

"We will come then."

I was about to go, for with this conversation we risked discovery. But Goyenne asked, "Do you have a knife, little sister?"

I slid my flint-bladed weapon through the opening, and Goyenne concealed it as I had done within the fold of her moccasin. She said no more.

I murmured, "You must eat. You will need strength for what lies ahead."

Goyenne nodded, and I dropped to my belly and began my fearful creep and freeze back to the dark fissure.

The ascent was of longer duration and harder to manage than the descent. But as the sky began to lighten I returned to the hidden scouts and to a sight that filled me with all the horror I had buried. Golahka sat holding Pocito tight across the chest, his knife pressed against the warrior's throat. A thin trickle of blood ran down Pocito's neck. Well could I see why it was needed. Without it, nothing could have stopped Pocito leaping into the canyon to save his wife.

Heads pressed together, we sat in council.

"The sunrise that follows this is the day they worship. All but the guards that stand at the top of the canyon go in."

"Then our warriors must spend their strength on these," Sotchez said.

"We will be in the valley, waiting," Chodini murmured. "When we have confined our enemy within the building, strike then."

Sotchez grunted his assent, and laying his hand on Pocito's shoulder said, "Brother, you shall come with me." It was a command, not a request, and together they slipped away to gather our force.

The remaining scouts waited, motionless. I cursed that I had not thought to find a way of filling my water vessel, for it was near empty and the day would be hot. I rationed myself, taking one small mouthful when my thirst grew too great. By the time the sun was directly above us, my water was gone. Golahka saw, and wordlessly shared his supply with me; and thus, as the long day progressed, we both went thirsty.

At nightfall we moved. The great hand of Ussen cast clouds across the moon as Pocito and Sotchez joined us once more. I felt the unseen presence of many warriors, concealed amongst the rocks, waiting for the light of dawn. Sotchez had a bundle tied to his belt. I knew not what it contained, but was certain that it meant death for the men below.

"I will climb upon the roof," he said, indicating the dwelling place of their god. A tree grew beside it that would give an easy way up. "It is but mud. I will pick a hole through it."

Chodini nodded. Our assault was planned thus: Golahka and Punte were to bar the doors once all the Mexicans were inside the building. This would signal the moment for our warriors to attack the guards at the top of the canyon. Pocito, Chodini and myself were to free the captives.

This time, I carried all my weapons and could not then fit within the concealing crevice. I, like the others, must climb down the rock face and take my agreed position behind the dwelling where the captives were imprisoned. While the Mexicans slept, we descended. It took much time, but it was done without detection, for none can move with such silent stealth as the Apache. When the wide sky began to flush red we were in our places.

I had curled myself tight between two boulders that stood at the rear corner of the captives' dwelling. From here I could see the house of their god.

At first light, a Mexican crossed the valley floor towards the building where Sotchez crouched, hidden in the roof. He was dressed in a hooded robe that hung from his shoulders and flapped as he walked like a vulture sidling towards a corpse. He entered and soon afterwards a great clanging filled the valley, the sound bouncing from rock to rock as the bell swung in its tower. I feared that Sotchez would surely be deafened.

Thus roused, fresh guards emerged and went to replace those of the night watch. Others hastened towards the building. It was as Goyenne had said: one by one each man removed his hat and filed inside. There remained but two guards on the valley floor – those who stood in front of the captives' dwelling, preventing their escape.

And then I saw the son of Pocito being led by the hand to worship the tortured god. His face was tight with anguish. As he passed the dwelling which housed the Chokenne women, he turned towards the window, looking for his mother, but the Mexican leading him gave his arm a sharp tug, and spoke harsh words of reprimand. The boy had the look of Tazhi. I could not let him go to his death. Neither could I save him, for to act now would be to pour all our lives into the laps of our enemy.

Yet I could give him warning.

Lifting my hands to my lips, I gave the cry of a mountain bird that dwelt high in the ranges of the

Chokenne, not here in the dusty heat of this canyon. The Mexican cares little for living things: I knew the man who led him would not even notice the call. But if the boy's soul were truly Apache, he would hear it.

His small body stiffened as he walked. He missed a step, and stumbled. He had heard. He knew of our presence, but there was enough of the warrior in him to know not to turn and look. And now his fate was in his own hands.

He was led into the church; the doors were pulled shut. At once, Golahka and Punte slid out from the side of the building to bar them. But before they could do so, a piping wail erupted from within.

"¡Quiero miar!"

I knew not the words, but could see from the great haste with which the doors were flung open and the boy was ejected from the building, clutching at his groin, that he had convinced his captors he was desperate to urinate. He came out from that place quickly. He came out alone.

Once more, the doors were closed. Forgetting caution, the boy ran to where I had concealed myself and threw himself against me joyfully, hot tears coursing down his cheeks. Before the guard who stood beside the captives' door could move to investigate, the body of a Mexican arced through the air from the top of the canyon, thudding into the dust, an arrow buried in his chest. The warriors had silently commenced their assault.

The guard stepped back and stared in astonishment as his comrade fell to earth. That slow reaction cost him his life, for at once Goyenne reached through the barred window and, seizing his hair, pulled back his head and drew my flint-bladed knife across his throat. Pocito plunged his into the belly of the other.

Thereafter, battle noise shook the narrow canyon. When the Mexicans realized they were under attack, cracks of gunfire split the air from above, and alerted those within the building.

Golahka and Punte wedged the doors tight shut even as the Mexicans within began to hammer upon them. From inside came shouts of anger and fear. There was a muffled explosion that I later learnt was the sound of a chilli bomb, and Sotchcz appeared on the roof without the bundle at his waist. Shouts changed to gasping coughs and groans of desperation as the bomb brought choking death with each indrawn breath. At last there was naught but silence.

The single shots that had been fired by the Mexicans in defence of their gold became triumphant volleys, for our warriors had finished their task and now fired into the air with their captured guns. Our attack had been swift and successful:

all the Mexicans lay dead, and we had lost not one warrior, not one captive.

Blinking, the women and children staggered into the light. It was a joy to see Chodini embrace his daughter, and lift his grandson high in the air, and watch Sotchez enfold his wife and son in his loving arms. They were weak with hunger and hard labour and could not walk the long distance to the Chokenne range. We took horses and mules that the freed captives might ride, and bound the smallest children to their mothers, so that they would not fall.

I watched Pocito lift his wife tenderly onto the back of a fine spotted mare. She shrank from his touch, and sat with dead eyes, staring straight ahead. Pocito flinched as if she had struck him. Yet when he placed his daughter on the horse in front of her, she clutched at the girl, as though she could prevent her drowning in the horror that engulfed her. Her son was put behind, his arms about his mother's waist, giving such comfort as he could. I saw that these children alone would keep Denzhone amongst the living. To be shamed – as she had been by the Mexicans – was unbearable. Had her children not held her, Pocito's wife would have taken a knife, severed her vessels, and emptied out her life upon the earth.

*   *   *

No eager boys waited to take the warriors' horses when we returned to the Chokenne camp, for they lay slain upon the red earth. Lacking them, the tribe was deeply wounded: who would now fill the places of the warriors as they grew old?

Yet even as they mourned, there was happiness amongst the captives, who rejoiced in their freedom. The trees rustled with content; the spring babbled in greeting; the land thrilled beneath the horses' feet to feel its people come home.

Upon our arrival, a mule was butchered and fires were lit to roast its meat. Ishta, who had trained beside me, had now completed his fourth journey, and was made a warrior. I had returned from my third, and knew well that with one more such expedition I too would be admitted to the council. My heart beat loud with excitement that I had come so far towards achieving my goal. I ached with impatience for the next time I should ride as a novice. And yet how could I wish for another fight such as this to come quickly?

After all had eaten, Sotchez spoke of the raid, telling the old men who had remained in the camp of our deeds. He spoke my name, honouring me for my part in it. I kept my eyes to the ground, for even while I gloried in his praise, I could not help but think that if I was raised so high in his esteem, a vengeful spirit might be tempted to cast me down.

But Sotchez's account was swiftly over, and the warriors' conversation moved to other things.

There was much talk of the White Eyes.

The camp we had seen when we raided cheese from Mexico had now become a great fort that squatted at the feet of the Chokenne range. Fort Cross, the White Eyes named it. Sotchez was at peace with these men; indeed, he had kept them supplied with firewood during the winter. But he was puzzled by their strange ways.

"They are like misguided children!" he said with a great laugh bursting from his chest. "They say the land is theirs! That they were given it long ago by the Mexicans!"

He shook his head, chuckling at their idiocy. Mirth spread amongst the warriors, for all knew such a thing was not possible: this land was created for the Apache. It was not for the Mexicans to give.

"How could any think to trade land? One may as easily exchange a blanket for the clouds, or a basket for the sky!" said Sotchez.

Chodini did not join in with the laughter. He sat silent, and did not speak of the humiliation he had endured at the White Eyes' hands. He would not open the wound by laying it before his fellows. Besides, the men at Fort Cross were not those at

Fort Andrews; we thought them separate tribes, and one could not be answerable for the actions of the other, no more than the Black Mountain tribe were responsible for the actions of the Chokenne.

But Chodini surely would not rest until he had taken revenge against them. Fear for my people clutched at my heart, holding it in its tight, cold fist. I trembled at what it might cost my tribe to have such an enemy at the very edge of our mountains – an enemy who had seemingly emptied the plains of the deer we fed upon. An enemy well armed, and plentiful, who could press us from the north even as the Mexicans did from the south. Thus squeezed, how were we to survive?

We stayed but one night amongst the Chokenne. At dawn, taking our portion of the mules, horses and ammunition we had captured from the Mexicans, we departed. But before I mounted, I found Paso at my elbow, daughter of the old man who had spoken to me of my father.

"He has gone to the Happy Place," she said softly.

It came as no surprise. Paso had been amongst the captives, and without her to tend to his needs, Danzih had turned his face to the tepee wall and slipped from the living earth.

"Last time... You had gone before he found the chance to talk with you again. He wished you to have this." She pressed something into my hand. "He said you would know from whose breast he had pulled it. He said it would have meaning for you."

It was an arrow. He could only have taken it from the body of my father. Its head was flint, its tail split with feathers to ease its flight, its shaft striped with red ochre. Recognition of it sent a wave of icy shock flooding through me. I kept my eyes averted from Paso's curious stare as I tried to quell the sickness that rose in my throat.

I knew who had fashioned it. Had I not spent long mornings of my childhood sitting beside him learning the skill of its creation? How was I to understand this new strangeness?

It seemed my father had been slain by his own arrow.

Despite the many troubles that snapped at the heels of my people, we retained our love of celebration. When we returned, triumphant, to our Black Mountain camp, there were many days of joyful feasting.

While we were in Mexico, Chee had come across a great nest of bees hanging high upon a rock. With arrows he had shot it down, letting it fall upon an outstretched hide, and with delight all now shared in eating acorn cakes dripping with the sweet honey.

"A hard time you have had of it, staying safely at home," Golahka teased him, for Chee's skin swarmed with bee stings. "You should have come with us. None of our war party suffered such injury as you."

"Save perhaps Siki," called Chodini. "Who has skinned her legs as deftly as she skins rabbits!"

I laughed, and at once began to cough, choking on my cake. Chee, placing his arm about my shoulders, thumped me hard on the back while merriment rippled amongst the warriors. When I had recovered my breath, I turned once more to speak with Golahka, but found that – swiftly and silently – he had gone.

In our absence, Zani, sister of Huten, had passed from girl to woman with her first flow of blood. With the return of our chief, her womanhood ceremony took place. Her father was dead, but her grandfather was not, nor her uncles, and thus there were many older relatives to provide all that was needed for the ritual.

By the grey light before sunrise, the men erected the ceremonial tepee. I was amongst those who gathered to watch them fasten scented boughs to the frame, and partly cover it in hides. As they worked, they sang the songs and prayers of this

217

most sacred rite. Huten's voice rang high and clear above the men's lower tones, his joyful pride in his sister carrying skywards to the stars that now faded before the rising sun.

In the centre of the tepee, a fire hole was dug. Beside the fire, blankets were spread that Zani and the women of her family would later sit upon. Opposite would sit the medicine man. An opening was left for those who would come and receive the blessings that Ussen would bestow through Zani during the four days of the ceremony, for at this time Zani would be a sacred figure: she would become one with White Painted Woman, the Mother of all Apache. Ussen would speak to her.

As soon as the tepee was complete, the men and women of the tribe gathered, standing in a wide circle around it. Chodini was magnificently attired in deerskin, a blanket of black and red draped from one shoulder, and wearing richly beaded moccasins. The women of Zani's family and the medicine man took their places within the tepee. When the sun crested the mountains, Zani's grandfather lifted his face to the east and raised his arms in prayerful song.

Then Zani came forth from her mother's tepee, and walked proud across our camp. She had been bathed and her hair washed in the crushed root of the yucca. Fragrant and soft, it hung loose about her shoulders as she came, carrying two lighted torches, dressed in the beautiful pale buckskin robes of the womanhood ceremony. Long had her mother laboured at sewing these robes. Much sinew had Huten been made to chew to soften it for the stitching – for many moons it had not been possible to pass him by without seeing the steady motion of his constantly grinding jaws. Now the work was rewarded. Zani's mother's eyes gleamed – moist with unshed tears – to see her daughter look so fine. A necklet hung upon Zani's breast, but its bright beads were dimmed by her shining beauty.

Beside me, Chee gasped at the sight of her. It seemed but days since Zani had been a girl who played and ran in the dust with the children. Now her face knocked breath from the chests of the men and boys who looked upon her. Naite's eyes burned with longing, and I was sure that Zani's womanhood ceremony would be swiftly followed by her marriage. Naite was nephew to Chodini; the match would be a welcome one for her family. And – proud warrior though he was – Naite was brimful of kindness; he would be a good brother to Huten.

Zani entered the ceremonial tepee and bent to light the sacred fire. Then, kneeling before the medicine man, she received the pollen upon her face that was a symbol of fertility. And now a long line of those who sought healing began to enter, filing past her to receive the blessings of Ussen.

I joined the line, and when my time came, I stood before her. Zani laid her hands on my skinned legs and at once I felt Power course through me. My heated flesh cooled, and the jangling nerves that had throbbed and kept me from sleep for many days eased and vanished.

For four days our tribe feasted and danced. For four nights the men's feet pounded in the dance of the mountain spirits. They leapt in the firelight while others sang and beat upon drums and set the mountains ringing.

Then came the social dances, when any woman could choose herself a partner and oblige the man to pay her – with meat or hides – for the privilege. Much mirth was there when Zani's aged aunt fell upon the blushing Ishta and compelled him to join her in the shuffling step around the fire. I was content to watch, for I did not wish to call down gossip on my head by choosing a partner. I could perhaps have danced with Chee, for he was as a brother to me, but in truth he had eyes for none but Zani and I did not wish to disturb his reverie.

And so I sat, wrapped in a blanket alongside the singers, lifting my voice to the black sky and feeling my spirit fly beside it. The dancers moved in a circle around the leaping flames, and it seemed to me that they were at the centre of many circles that wound outwards from this core: that of the swirling seasons and the spinning stars and the endless dance of life and death. Here was happiness. Here was harmony. Here was peaceful content. My people, beloved by the land that fed us, dancing in exultation beneath the moon.

But even amid this joy, a discordant note clanged within me. It started softly – a mere buzzing in my ears – but became louder and would not be silenced. Try as I might, I could not stop its noise, and it rendered my song tuneless.

I could not forget the arrow of my father. I carried it wrapped in a cloth inside my quiver. Alone of our tribe, my father had painted the shaft of his arrows with ochre. There could be no doubt that it was his. My father had ever loved to gamble. It was not hard to see how it had come into another's hands, for had I not lost a whole quiver on a game of shinny? I knew not to whom it had fallen, and yet it seemed likely that it would have been won by a Black Mountain warrior.

I had been slow to examine the thoughts the

arrow called forth, burying them deep inside my mind as ones too dark to look upon. I could evade them no longer.

I had never questioned why a party of warriors containing Golahka – a war shaman – had wandered so blindly into an ambush, but I did so now, and saw that it could only have happened if there had been some great failing on the part of the scouts. Potro. Or my father. Why he – who had been so skilled – should have failed thus was impossible to know. But certain it was that his actions had not gone unseen. I knew that Punte had watched, and told Keste of it. And now I had to accept that perhaps there were others who had knowledge of it. Ozheh, Torrez and Biketsin had returned from the ambush. So had Golahka. When I considered the arrow I saw that my father's cowardice had not gone unpunished. Someone – a warrior of my own tribe, perhaps one who even now sat and mingled his voice in song with mine – had fired the arrow that killed my father.

Time passed, and still Chodini took no vengeance for the insult he had received from the White Eyes. Faint murmurs of disquiet arose from some of the young men, who began to whisper that the chief had become old and wearied with battle. In truth, he was aged. But his prowess was undimmed, and it was not weariness that stayed his hand. It was the vow of brotherhood he had made with the White Eyes. He had given his word. Chodini was a proud man, and an honourable one. To break his word would have been an act akin to hacking off his own limb.

In those moons of uneasy peace, our tribe was increased in number by the arrival of two Hilaneh warriors. They knew well the prowess of Chodini and Golahka and sought to ride beside them. These warriors were welcomed as our own. But with them they brought many tales: disturbing tales that set our teeth on edge.

The territory of the Hilaneh is far to the east, separated from the range of the Dendhi by a broad desert plain. It seemed that into their fertile hills so many White Eyes had come that to avoid them the Hilaneh were forced into ever smaller corners of their own land. As if this were not hard enough, these settlers had made an agreement in which they promised to protect the Mexicans against the Apache!

This tale passed from mouth to mouth with angry confusion.

"Do they not know of the Mexicans' treachery?" asked Chodini.

"They do. Our chief has told them often. Was he not a child at Bavisco?"

All knew to what the Hilaneh warrior referred. Many summers ago, members of his tribe had been invited to feast with the Mexicans in the town of Bavisco. When all had taken their places, the Mexicans offered a great spread of food, and stood watching as the tribe satisfied their hunger.

The food was poisoned.

Warrior, woman and child alike died. Near fifty of the Hilaneh had ended their lives in tortured spasms.

"Has not the Mexican always sought to take Apache lives?" asked Chodini, perplexed. "Why should the White Eyes then side with the Mexicans against us: we, who have offered the White Eyes nothing but friendship and welcome?"

None could answer his question, for indeed what could be said? All agreed with Golahka as he commented, "The ways of these people are strange indeed. We should keep far from them."

To preserve the peace, we shunned contact with the White Eyes, staying away from the trails they made across the plains. While the Apache makes his way by following the mountains, the White Eyes ride beside the rivers in our dry country as if terrified to leave them. They were but guests on our land; Ussen did not whisper to them of where to find the water that lay hidden beneath the earth. They must cling to the springs and watercourses. Thus it seemed an easy task to avoid them.

Of Keste, there had been no sighting. It was more than fifteen moons since he had gone from our camp, and I had ceased to listen for the twang of his bowstring. I believed he had long since left the Black Mountain range, and perhaps joined with the groups of wild young renegades that roamed the mountains near to the border with Mexico. I could not believe Dahtet would fare well living such a life, and my heart sorrowed for her.

As the earth lay basking in the heat of summer, I rode to the upland plain to hunt rabbits with no thought of danger. Many of the women and children had gone east to harvest the mescal that grows in the rocky foothills, the baked hearts of which would help feed the tribe throughout the winter. They were accompanied by many warriors, for the capture of the women and children of the Chokenne was still fresh in our minds. Thus neither Golahka nor Chodini was in our camp when I set forth alone.

I hunted well that day; the horse I rode had long

since known the ways of our tribe, and ran after rabbits with no bidding. I butchered the creatures there on the grass, spilling their guts on the ground for the vultures that the meat would not sour. Tying their back legs together with a thread of sinew, I slung my kill from the shoulder of my horse and turned for home.

As I began to descend the mountain trail, I saw smoke rising from the flat desert in the west. It was a great distance from the White Eyes' settlement so it could not be a fire lit by them. Full well I knew that our women and children had travelled east – and besides, any fires they made would be of dry wood and lit in deep arroyos that they would not alert our enemies to where they camped – so neither did it belong to them.

This fire had been lit with green wood to create much smoke: a signal fire. One of our people was in distress. My heart leapt within me, and, throwing aside the rabbits I had slain, I rode at once towards it.

The person who lights a signal fire will retreat to a hidden place where they may watch who comes in answer, for the smoke can as well be seen by an enemy as a friend. On reaching the fire, I expected to wait long for the person who had made it. I jumped from my horse, throwing the reins down beside a pile of rags seemingly heaped beside the fire to feed it, and began to look about me.

It was only when the heaped rags stirred and a clawed hand reached beseechingly towards me that I knew my mistake.

It was a woman. A woman who had not the strength to crawl away and conceal herself. A cloth covered her head, but as her eyes sought mine it fell back. I started in shock: her nose was split open with a knife. The wound was fresh; it had perhaps occurred four or five sunrises since, for although dried blood had crusted upon her neck, a new flow now began to ooze forth.

I felt no stir of recognition. I did not know her. For many thudding heartbeats I stared, horrified, upon the ruined face. And then she spoke.

"Siki…" Her voice was cracked with thirst and as faint as the hiss of an arrow. But it set my ears ringing and my heart pounding as if Ussen had roared my name from the mountain tops. "Siki. Do you not know me, sister?"

Tears I could not shed for Tazhi now ran for Dahtet. More easily could I have borne finding her dead than seeing her like this – her body destroyed, the gentle soul within her crushed. She had fled with nothing – not even a vessel for water – and made the journey homewards alone and unarmed. It had cost her dear. She was little more than a dried-out shell.

Burning off its thorns in the ashes of the fire, I split leaves of the prickly pear and laid them across Dahtet's wounded face to soothe it. A few sips of water and a mouthful of dried meat was all she could take before her eyes clouded with weariness. When I lifted her onto my horse, she was light as a child, her bones brittle as twigs. I rode behind her, her head thrown back against my shoulder, my arms about her waist to stop her falling; she was so weakened with hunger and thirst that she could not sit unaided.

I had ridden fast across the plain that morning, but our return was slow. The horse could do no more than walk with us riding thus, and the sun had already dipped below the horizon when at last we entered our camp.

The women had also returned from the east, for the tepees burst with laughter and life. Everyone fell silent on seeing Dahtet. They could not yet view her face, hidden as it was beneath its binding, but all surmised who she was as I stopped beside her family's tepee, and an astonished murmur rippled through the camp.

I had barely laid her unconscious body upon the

warm hides and left her in the care of her weeping mother, when her father's roar of outrage tore the night air. He stood amongst the warriors, arms outstretched towards the stars. "I will avenge this wrong," he swore to Ussen. "I will hunt Keste down. I will kill him."

"No." The voice was quiet. Hard, cold as the steel-bladed sword. It was Punte, father of Keste. "You will not. He is my son. I will do it."

Dahtet did not know what the men planned.

In the days that followed, she kept to her tepee and did not see the warriors' brows furrowed with anger, nor the stone face of Punte, nor hear her own father murmuring to Golahka of the vengeance he would take. Dahtet said she was too weak to leave the pile of hides upon which she lay, and she refused to be carried into the sun's healing warmth. In truth she feared to have the tribe look upon her ruined face. Even before me she could scarce lift her head and meet my eyes for the weight of heartache and shame that burdened her.

Keste had marked her as one who had betrayed her husband. An adulteress.

Her innocence was not in doubt. But innocence would not heal her wounds, nor soothe away the horror of her mutilation.

Only in the concealing night did she at last begin to whisper of what had befallen.

"Between the mountains of the Chokenne and the Dendhi there is a range that extends into Mexico. It was here that we settled."

"None could find you," I told her. "Keste was sought, but no trace of you was discovered." I did not tell her of his attack on me. I could not add to her woes.

"We were well hidden," she sighed. "In a valley – a mountain scooped hollow by the great hand of Ussen. There is but one way in, and that is concealed beneath a great slab of stone. A single juniper tree clings to a rock above it. Truly, Siki, I felt as though I had entered the Happy Place when we found it. There we remained. We were safe. Keste was content. Then others came: three young men who had also gone from their tribes. They were wild, Siki, and they challenged him, but Keste bested them all. He is a fine warrior." Dahtet could not keep the pride from her voice. "And now they look upon him as their chief."

I bit my tongue to catch the sour words that wished to fall. Keste's ambition had burned so bright that his own tribe could not contain him: he had to fashion a new world about himself in which he could shine as leader. A pretty picture indeed.

"It was Keste who hurt you?" I was in no doubt, for well I knew his ungovernable temper. But still I wished to hear it from the mouth of Dahtet.

"Yes." She tore her own heart out admitting it. "He became jealous. He thought I looked with admiration upon the others. I did not, Siki, I swear it. Yet still he punished me." Her voice became the smallest of whispers. "Often he went away hunting, raiding. Seven sunrises ago, he returned swaying, and I knew he had drunk much Mexican liquor. He said I had lain with other men in his absence." Dahtet was filled with confusion. "But even if I had wished it, how could I have done so? The other men had gone with him when he rode. I was alone."

"Do not seek reason in the actions of Keste," I murmured. "He has surely tipped into madness."

"He has not!" Even now, Dahtet leapt to defend him.

"To hurt an innocent woman? Is this justice?" I asked hotly.

"No indeed." Dahtet began to weep. "And I am marked for ever! All will call me faithless."

"They will not. Your people know your worth." I spoke soothingly, but even now Dahtet felt no ill will towards Keste.

"Siki," she said falteringly, "I have thought that perhaps his jealousy came from great love. For does

231

not love make men do foolish things? I think perhaps it was love of me that made him do this. Might it not be so?"

How could I answer such a question? Her tone begged me, pleaded with me to turn the universe on its head. It was easier to say that we walked on the stars and that Mother Earth hung above our heads than believe that this mutilation was an act of love!

And yet how could I say aught else but "Perhaps." The word stuck like a knife in my throat.

Satisfied with this lie, Dahtet lay back upon the hides. Soon her soft breathing told me she was asleep.

And then in the darkness I knew that her father was not. He had heard all. His breathing had quickened with fury. Fury, and sudden excitement, for Dahtet had, all unknowing, told him where he would find Keste.

I did not wish to go. Many moons before – when I had first felt the chill of Keste's hatred – I had made a solemn vow that I would not harm one of my own tribe. And yet when Golahka came to me, it seemed I had little choice.

"Four will track him," said Golahka. "The fathers of Dahtet and Keste. Our chief. Myself. We would have sought him long before, but knew not where to look. He will cause more harm if he remains free. He must be killed. For justice. You know it, Siki, do you not?"

I could not answer. My mouth had become dry as the desert dust. My heart pounded.

"Dahtet would not wish it," I whispered.

"Dahtet will not know."

"Yes!" I raged. "She will know. How could she not? Did not all hear her father's vow of vengeance? The women will tell her."

Golahka laid his hand upon mine and set my spirit trembling. "She will not know until we are gone. It will be too late then for her to do aught."

I shook my head. It was not Dahtet warning Keste that troubled me, but the knowledge of how sharp her pain would be, how great her anger, if she knew I rode against him. I would not betray her. I could not do such a thing.

"I cannot come. I will not."

"It is Chodini's request." Golahka paused awhile to let his words settle in my head. My chief wished me to ride beside him. There could be no greater honour. And it would be my fourth journey. On my return, I would be a warrior.

"To refuse your chief is also a betrayal, is it not, Siki?" Golahka's eyes fixed me, glinting darkly. "You cannot deny the justice of this task. Is not justice of

233

greater import than loyalty to one who has been blinded by love? If Keste remains upon the living earth we must always be looking over our shoulders, waiting for him to strike. Let us end it now."

I could do nothing but nod my assent even as my stomach churned with misgiving. And then the strangeness of Chodini requesting that a novice girl ride beside him made me ask, "Why does he wish me to come?"

"We have need of you: of your Power." Golahka's voice was hard. Cold. His eyes met mine once more, full of a challenge which he dared me to meet. "Besides," he added, "we must make use of you. Your presence will draw Keste forth. It is you who will bait the trap."

Some summers before, a mountain lion had roamed amongst the rocks of our home. There are many such creatures in the hills, but it is rare indeed for them to attack our people. Yet this beast was aged, with a wounded leg that rendered it impossible to hunt deer as it had once done. Instead, it attacked a boy – older brother to Chee – seizing him by his head as he played with his friends in the hills and dragging him, lifeless, away. Chee's grieving father, Biketsin, determined to catch and kill the beast, and thus he brought his dog to the very place where we had played, and tied it to a stake to tempt the creature forth. For five sunrises he watched and waited, and the dog grew thin at the end of its rope.

On the sixth sunrise Biketsin returned to our camp carrying the bloody hide of the mountain lion. The dog was not at his heels.

Chee and I had gone searching for it, and found the dog still tied to its rope, its side slashed open, its insides spilt upon the earth. Being children we had wept for it, shedding perhaps more tears for the animal than we had for Chee's brother, for to mourn a dog is simple.

I recalled its glazed eyes as our grim band rode silently towards Keste's hidden valley. It had seemed to me that even in death the dog's terror had not abated. It had risen from the corpse in heated waves, strong as the scent of decay. And now my own throat was tight and dry, as though Golahka had placed a rope about it, and now bade me stand and wait.

There was more here than I understood. I had never seen the face of Golahka so stern. I could not interpret what made his eyes into dark, dead pools, and his mouth a tight, hard line. Why had he spoken of betrayal? When I considered it, my belly contracted with fear – not to face Keste, but that

Golahka knew of my father's cowardly flight. In my reluctance to go, had I perhaps ignited the flame of suspicion in his mind? Did he doubt my courage? Did he seek to test me?

While I sought to understand what lay behind his coldness, suddenly a new and terrible dread gripped my mind.

Had Golahka himself fired the arrow that had slain my father?

Golahka had ever been my mentor, my teacher, my friend. But a great chasm had opened up between us, and I knew not how to cross it.

Anguished, sick with foreboding, I scarce saw where we rode. My head was ever bowed with the weight of fear that Golahka had poured upon me. I knew only that Chodini tracked the path Dahtet had taken when she fled. I took little heed, for it was an easy task: her trail was spotted with blood. When Chodini raised his hand and made a sign for us to halt, I saw in the distance the place where a lone juniper tree stood clinging to a rock. The valley was indeed concealed. Had Dahtet not spoken of it, even the most skilled tracker would have ridden past thinking the trail lost and cold.

And now Golahka came to me, his face as hard as the rock that the tree's roots desperately clung to.

"Go on alone. Do not conceal yourself. Tempt

Keste forth. If he comes not, light a fire beneath the tree. Use green wood. Make much smoke. Signal him. When he comes, tell him you bring word from his wife."

"Word?" I asked. My mind was empty. I could not invent a lie. "What word?"

The father of Dahtet said quietly, "Tell him she is with child." From his eyes I knew he spoke truth. A hiss of breath escaped from Punte, and I realized he had not known of this until now.

"Very well," I said.

"We four will separate. I will cross the high rocks and come upon the place from behind that line of trees," said Chodini.

"I will go by the lower trail," offered Punte.

The father of Dahtet would mirror Chodini's route, and come from the other side of the valley.

"I will follow the stream." Golahka's voice was hoarse; he would not meet my eyes. Suddenly I saw that he was afraid. I had never known him thus. My own teeth clenched in response and I found I could not speak. Digging my heels into my horse's side, I rode forth noisily along the trail.

I snapped twigs, and sent stones rolling from the scree. With agonizing slowness I moved across Keste's land. He knew these valleys, these rocks; I did not. I could not be certain he had not watched, hidden, as we parted our ways. Even as I clattered along, he might be slitting the throat of my chief. Of Golahka.

And as I rode a fresh uncertainty snapped at my heels. We had accepted that Punte would ride beside us. None questioned his honour, his belief in justice. But were we right to do so? Was it not possible that he had ridden not to kill but to save Keste? Would he betray his tribe to save his son?

I hesitated, pausing on the track, thinking to warn Golahka.

But I did not. I could not. For there, sudden on the mountain trail before me, was Keste. Beside him stood his father, Punte, gazing at me with unwavering eyes, his expression an unfathomable mask.

Keste smiled. A baring of teeth. A grimace that betrayed his madness. The gun gleaming in his hand was pointed at my chest.

"And so you all come," he said, his voice soft and sweet. "The girl warrior rides willingly as bait towards her death. I saw that it would be so."

"I bring word from your wife," I answered.

Keste laughed. "You lie. You come to kill me." He sat idly upon a rock, his finger never moving from the trigger. "You see, Siki, I have Power too. I foresaw your coming. I have watched you these past days and have seen what you planned. And now

I use my Power to do you harm. Golahka is right to be afraid." He nodded towards the juniper. "They go to the tree; they think to protect you there. But look! I am here. Here, where they cannot defend you."

I looked to Punte to intervene, but he said naught.

"You think my father will save you?" Keste laughed long and loud. "My father, who even now urges me to flee to safety? You think he will not put his son's life above all else?"

"Dahtet carries your child." I said it to delay the pulling of his trigger, but at this Keste laughed once more – a great, ringing roar that must alert the others. Punte looked about him, but Keste did not.

"Not mine," he said. "She spoke many loving lies, but she was faithless. She thought to make a mockery of me. As you did."

I could not keep my silence. "I did not! It was your own pride that betrayed you; your own folly that took you into exile."

Anger flickered across Keste's face and I knew my words had struck him. "You think me foolish? You? A girl whose father fled weeping from the fight? Who deserted his brothers? A stripling girl who now dares to ride beside those same warriors?

You dishonour the whole tribe by doing so. Chodini is a woman to allow it. I will not have such a chief. I make my own tribe."

At this I could not help but laugh bitterly. "Ah yes. Keste, leader of renegades; chief of outcasts. How proud your father must be!"

Punte flinched at this gibe, but still did not speak.

"Do not talk to me so!" Keste's voice was tight with threat. "Be silent! You are but a girl!"

I would not obey him, though it would provoke him to attack. "A girl, yes. A stripling girl that has always bested you."

"You will not do so again. Nor trick me either. I have learnt that lesson well." Keste smiled – a twisted grin of pleasure in the harm he would now inflict. "It is time for you to join your brother. Perhaps your clever hands can fashion him a new head."

He fired his weapon.

My horse reared in fright, and I fell back on the hard ground. The breath was knocked from me and I lay gasping, wondering where I bled, waiting for the blow that would drive me from the living earth.

And then I heard the voice of Punte, dry as the winter leaves. "You are not slain, Siki. Get up."

Punte stood over his son, his bloodied war club

dangling from one hand. Keste's cheek was caved in with the force of the blow, and his eyes blazed with shock and pain.

I got to my feet, and as I did so, Golahka came running. When he saw Punte standing over his injured son, the great warrior let out a breath so deep that he had to steady himself against the rock.

Despite his hurt, Keste would not be still. He spat blood, and though his tongue was thick, his lips swollen, he managed to say petulantly, "Why must you take her part? Has she bewitched you all?"

"Be silent," Punte told him.

"She is not your kin! Who is she that you should side with her? I am your son!"

"Siki is of my tribe," Punte answered. "And you are my son no more."

"You disown me?" Keste's voice had risen to a high, hysterical pitch.

"You disown yourself." Punte's reply was no more than a whisper. "You condemn yourself. With every word you seal your own fate. There must be justice."

As he looked upon his father, Keste seemed to shrink. And now he was deathly silent.

Chodini came upon us then, with the father of Dahtet, driving Keste's renegade band before them. Drunk on Mexican liquor and lying in a deep

241

slumber, they had only been roused by a jab from the point of Chodini's gun. Their capture was an easy task.

All were allowed the opportunity to speak. To defend themselves.

They did not.

None asked for mercy. The renegades cursed, boasting of their Power and the evil they would call down on the heads of Chodini and his tribe.

"Witches all," pronounced my chief. There was a dreadful pause as we waited for the words we knew would come next. "They must die."

At this, Keste spoke, his voice cold with menace. "Do not think you will be free of me," he told Chodini. "I shall not go to sport and hunt in the Happy Place." His eyes met mine as he sent forth his venom. "While you live, I will walk the living earth and cause you harm. My spirit shall stalk you. This does not end here."

These words held such horror that I could not answer. Well I knew that Keste would do as he said. Every moment of solitude would be haunted by him. His chill hatred would follow me always, smothering me in an enveloping mist. I would never be warm again; I would never be free.

Golahka spoke. "She bested you in life, Keste. You think it will be any different in death?"

Keste's eyes flashed with malice, and he struggled to throw off his father's restraining hand.

"Enough," Chodini commanded. "Let us finish this now. Siki, return to the horses. This is not for you to see."

Glad I was of it. I did not wish to watch this execution. I mounted my horse and turned to go. As I did so, Punte lifted his sagging head and braced his shoulders. His words were ripped from his throat.

"My chief, this task is mine."

Chodini gave his assent as I urged my horse forward.

I rode swiftly to where the other animals were hobbled, and there I slid from her back and fell, curling weakly upon the earth, for suddenly my body was seized with violent shaking. The air was yet warm; the sun still shone; but I shivered with shock, my teeth clacking noisily together as if I had plunged into an icy mountain stream.

When the warriors returned, they had the look of men sickened by what they had been forced to do. Punte's face was dark, frozen still as a mask. He walked as stiffly as the oldest of our tribe, as though he might crack at the slightest touch.

No one spoke. On the long days of our journey home none said a word.

Though I had known much sorrow and tasted much grief, I felt I had never looked upon its true face, nor heard its true sound, until I woke in the cold grey light that comes before the dawn and heard the soft sound of Keste's father crying. Punte, that brave warrior, was sobbing like a child.

No blaze of triumph gave me admission to the warrior council, no battle victory, no triumphant feast following a raid. But in hunting Keste I had ridden on my fourth such journey as a novice. Unless any now found fault with me, I was to be considered a warrior. An equal. Chodini talked quietly to the men, and none made any objection. And thus he came to me some days after our return, and embraced me.

"Now I must call you brother," he laughed. "The next time we fight, you shall be at my side." This is the way for the new warrior – to be amongst the leaders in battle to test courage and prove worth.

"Were you a young man you would now be free to marry, Siki," said Chodini. "You have no father to speak for you, but gladly I would do so, if you wish?"

"No," I answered at once. My thoughts were full of Tazhi. I would have no child. All else I could bear: I would suffer and struggle and be strengthened by it. But not this: I could not bring forth a child to see it slaughtered. This alone was unendurable.

Chodini seemed surprised by the passion of my answer. I did not explain. I could not frame the words without choking and I would not show weakness before my chief. I kept my eyes fixed upon the earth. Thus I did not see Chodini walk from me to where Golahka stood in the shadows, nor hear their murmured conversation. I did not see Golahka's eyes narrow as if with pain. Of this I was only told many moons later, by Dahtet. But by then it had ceased to matter.

Strange it felt to have achieved my task. I walked proud amongst the warriors, and was glad to call myself their equal. But in truth, I took less joy in it than most, for it had been bought with the heart's blood of Dahtet. Always her eyes – heavy with the accusation of betrayal – followed me about the camp. Often I felt a chill prickling my spine, and knew not whether it was Keste's restless spirit come to haunt me, or Dahtet's new-roused hatred.

I could not now rest in her family's tepee, and thus I began to fashion my own, bartering arrows and small game for hides with any who would trade with me. I made but a small framework, for it needed to house only myself. Even so, with all the hides I had gathered, a gaping hole remained. Nahasgah would have laughed at my ineptitude, but

I cursed myself that these homely skills ran so low in me, for I would be cold indeed when the winter winds blew.

I was rescued from discomfort by Dahtet's mother, Hosidah. She came quietly at sundown, a buffalo hide in her arms.

"A payment, daughter," she said. "For the rabbits you once gave."

"They were not worth so much!" I protested, but Hosidah shook her head.

"Take it as a gift then, if you will not accept a payment. Dahtet will never thank you. But we, her parents, know how great a debt we owe you," she said. Laying it down, she proceeded to set my clumsy work right.

A question had troubled me ever since Dahtet had first gone from the camp. I could not now know the answer from Dahtet, for she would have no more talk with me, and so I asked her mother, "Did she go willingly?"

"Oh yes," she answered.

"But to cause you such distress! And herself such shame! Why could Keste not have waited until he was made warrior? Then they could have wed with honour!" I sighed, shaking my head, and added, "I thought perhaps he had forced her into exile."

Hosidah gave a rueful smile. "Keste was Dahtet's

whole tribe: mother, father, brother, all. While he smiled on her, she cared for nothing else. This was love, misplaced though it was. You are a warrior, daughter. Do not expect to understand it."

But as I lay that night in my solitary tepee I was filled with the sudden, overwhelming knowledge that I understood Dahtet's feeling. Full well could I comprehend it. For – though we seemingly now stood on either side of a great canyon – I knew that Golahka had become whole tribe to me.

I was a warrior then, but I did not expect to be tested in battle for many moons. We had repaid the Mexicans for their treacherous attack at Koskineh; we had freed the Chokenne captives at Marispe. I thought that now a time of peace would come. With pleasure, I looked forward to racing on foot, and on horseback. I anticipated games of shinny, and long tales beside the fire.

But in thinking so, I had forgotten the White Eyes.

Such friendship as had once existed between our peoples grew thin, stretched tight as a bowstring.

I had avoided contact with these strangers since I had ridden with Chodini to trade at Fort Andrews many moons ago, but it was becoming harder to do so. They were drawn to our land like flies to fresh spilt blood, and like flies they swarmed and multiplied, so that soon we could not ride across the great land Ussen had given us without seeing their presence on every horizon. If I stood on any mountain top and looked about me I saw distant dwellings in every direction. Smoke rose from their many fires, so numerous that it seemed to me they would choke the clear sky. The sight gave me much distress, for I felt that these people would not give peace, no matter how much we longed for it.

There was another cause for my unease. Since Keste had been killed, Golahka had been strange and cold with me. Punte knew of my father's betrayal, and yet had trusted me above his son. But this was not so with Golahka. Many times I felt his gaze follow me about the camp. Often I would turn and see his black eyes slide swiftly away. I knew not why he watched me thus, and could only think that he looked on me with suspicion, lest I follow my father's cowardly path. For Golahka had heard the gasp of relief I had breathed unguarded when the Mexican cheese farmers had fled with their lives. Did he think I carried the seeds of my father's treachery in my blood? Did he watch for signs of those seeds growing in me? I dreaded that he would speak to me, for if he did I would have to ask him what he knew of my father's death.

I kept my fears caged within my breast; I thought I had twined together the strands Ussen had placed before me, and I now saw the shape of the whole. My father had gone ahead. By accident – I could not think it was by design – he had seen the Mexicans too late. I understood not why he fled, but was certain such a deed would have enraged any who saw it. I would not ask who had fired the red ochre arrow that killed him, for I feared the answer would be Golahka. It was knowledge I did not desire.

This, then, was the shape of what I saw. I could not know that this truth I had fashioned was as poor and lopsided as the jug I had made at Koskineh.

Ill crafted as it was, it caused a great awkwardness to grow between myself and Golahka, and I began to seek ways to avoid him. In doing so, I felt as though I plucked the living heart from my chest. My soul was threaded to his, and with each step I felt its tug. I ached with his absence, and was gripped by the same weary, irritable restlessness that had possessed me after the loss of Tazhi.

I took refuge in the company of Chee, for well I knew that the greater part of his heart had belonged to Zani since her womanhood ceremony. She had wed Naite and now carried his child, but Chee could not help his eyes growing big as a doe's whenever she passed near, though he never spoke of her. Thus we were as brother and sister; between us there could be no mistrust, no misunderstanding; and often in the days that followed we rode side by side in search of antelope and deer.

In the fading heat of late summer, Chee and I hunted together. By the time the sun began to sink we walked homewards with two antelope slung across our horses. But a new dwelling at the foot of the mountain track blocked our way: a small house, a fenced corral beside it with a few head of beef. I froze.

"White Eyes," I whispered, and turned to go by another path.

But Chee laughed, and led his horse forward. His good humour made him look kindly on all. "Why do you waste your strength on needless worry? We have nothing to fear. I wish to return to our camp, and this is the quickest way."

"Have you forgotten the insult the White Eyes gave to our chief?"

Chee stopped. "I have not. But that insult was not given by these people. These are farmers, not soldiers. Besides, those whom Chodini met at the spring had been drinking, had they not? All men are idiots when they have drunk much liquor. Chodini knows it." Chee looked at me confidently. "It is why he takes no revenge."

"Perhaps," I said uncertainly.

"It is so," declared Chee. "Come, Siki, let us pay a visit to these newcomers. I wish to taste their hospitality."

Without listening to my anxious protestations, he walked towards the dwelling.

I had never seen such terror, nor known so little cause for it.

Tethering his horse to a rough-hewn fence, Chee had boldly entered the dwelling, and sat himself smiling down on the beaten earth floor. I followed, for I felt I could do naught else.

It was dark inside, and briefly I was blinded. But as soon as my eyes grew accustomed to the deep shadow, I saw a yellow-haired woman standing with her back pressed flat to the wall, her hands frozen either side of her mouth, her eyes wide with fear. The mere sight of two Apache had reduced the woman to speechless horror. Beside her, clutching at her skirts and whimpering, were several small children.

I was shocked at the sight of so many offspring. An Apache woman has one child, followed by another after perhaps three or more summers. It is rare indeed for her to have more than four children in the whole course of her life. But this woman had so many children of such similar size that I thought perhaps the White Eyes gave birth to their babies in litters like dogs or rats.

Chee, who had learnt some of their tongue from the soldiers at Fort Andrews, spoke words of friendship. The woman made no answer. Chee's brow furrowed with confusion.

"Why does she not offer us food?" he said.

It is the Apache way that when strangers come, we give at once the best of what we have. It is the rule of hospitality to give freely to those who have need. And yet this woman made no move. Looking about him, Chee noticed a large cake – perhaps made from the strange white powder that Ozheh had once traded for – standing on a wooden box. He pointed, but the woman did not attempt to share it.

"Maybe she lacks meat," he suggested, reaching for the bag at his waist that he might offer her some.

Thinking perhaps that he reached for his knife, the woman made a sound – a high-pitched gasp that burst from her fear-pinched lips. She moved from the wall, thrusting the brood of children behind her as if to protect them.

"She dreads us," I said. "We must go."

But now Chee was angered by her fear for it insulted him. "Why should she dread us? We have done nothing! Why does she not give us food?"

"Perhaps it is not their custom."

"Then why is she upon our land if she will not follow our ways?" he demanded.

Chee stood, and put his hand forward to take the long cake that he might divide it in friendship between us. But the woman sprang wildly at it, and held it to her chest in one hand as though it were her precious babe. With the other she grasped the knife that had lain beside it, and made small stabbing motions at Chee as though to drive him away. Her eyes flashed with a look I had seen once before, and my heart sank in recognition. It was the outraged expression of the dark-haired Mexican I had seen long ago in a vision – he who had died defending his cattle from the Chokenne.

And now I knew why I mistrusted the White Eyes. Like the Mexican, they had no understanding that the bounty of Mother Earth was made for all to share. Instead they snatched, and grabbed, and hoarded more than their needs, piling it all into a great heap that they defended like snarling dogs. Did they not see that they thus deprived their fellow men of the means to fill their bellies? A strange, greedy race indeed that now walked amongst us!

"Come, Chee," I said, laying my hand upon his arm. "Let us go from here."

At last he came away, vexed that his friendly openness had been met with mistrust. "She looked upon me as if I were a snake!" he exclaimed as he loosed his horse and led it away up the mountain path. Chee's pride was much offended, but I was relieved this was all that had been hurt.

As we crested the hill, I saw a White-Eyed man far below us carrying two dead rabbits. Seeing us, he sped towards his dwelling. The woman came out calling, screaming, pointing in our direction. The man raised his gun, but we were already far from him and he did not trouble to waste his shot. We moved out of sight swiftly, and naught else followed. But I was certain that if we had stayed longer in that place – had the man returned from his hunt while we were within – we could not have left without bloodshed.

Chee, who had once welcomed the White Eyes, spoke no more of our land being large enough for all to dwell in. The woman's look of loathing irked him constantly, like a thorn embedded in his moccasin. And yet this was but a small occurrence: a bee sting.

Many worse hurts were daily being done to our brother tribes.

That summer, three Black Mountain warriors who had married into the Dendhi visited their parents in our camp. They brought their families, and from their mouths we heard many terrible tales.

The Dendhi had endured the settling of the White-Eyed soldiers. They had endured the coming of farmers who fenced the land as though it belonged to them. But they could not endure the arrival of those who mined for gold and silver, who hacked at Mother Earth and crawled in the wounds they had made, tongues lolling like hunger-maddened coyotes. A large settlement had sprung up at the edge of the Dendhi range and it had brought pain and suffering to many.

These miners were worse even than the soldiers: reckless, with wild and vicious tempers. Seemingly these barbarous men had nothing but contempt for the Apache. They paid no regard to whose land they walked upon; they brought Mexicans from across the border to grow their food as they would not gather their own, heedless of the insult given to our people.

Many skirmishes erupted: fights, arguments, small battles, each one started by the White Eyes.

A warrior had been shot, a woman shamed, a child slain. Each family had gone first to the White Eyes' chief to ask for justice. None was given. Thus each family took their own revenge, as is the Apache way. Ussen cares not for the squabbles of men: he trusts us to mete out punishment where it is needed.

As yet, the Dendhi were not roused to take the warpath, and though troubled by these tales, there was no thought that our tribes would join and fight the White Eyes together. It was only when great wrong was done to Chodini, our chief, that the Apache nation was provoked to war.

It happened thus.

Perhaps one moon after I had become a warrior, we were surprised by a lone man – a White Eyes – riding boldly into our camp bearing a flag of truce. He led behind him the fine stallion taken from Chodini some time before by the soldiers at the spring. This man sought Chodini. Dismounting from his horse and clasping my chief's hand in friendship, he at once began to address him in Apache.

"Brother, I come in peace. I bring your horse as a token of the goodwill between us. My own chief has much he wishes to discuss with you. He asks you to come and feast beside him. He camps on the plain and waits for your arrival. Bring your wives, your children. Come and share the bounty of the great white father."

It was a speech he had learnt with little understanding, for when Chodini replied, the man had to fall into Spanish once more. But I stood astounded that he knew any words of the Apache tongue and wondered how he had learnt them. I wondered too that he had entered our mountain home and found our hidden camp with seeming ease. Golahka looked as unsettled as I, and it gave Chodini cause to frown. But our chief was a man of peace and retained a vestige of goodwill towards these invaders. They had returned his horse: this, surely, was an act of friendship. So he agreed that he would bring his family to the White Eyes' encampment in two sunrises.

He did not go alone, and he did not go unarmed.

Ozheh, his son; Naichise, his brother; and Naichise's two sons – Naite and Parcohte – went with him. Zani remained within our camp, for being with child she did not like to ride so far from her own mother. Instead, Huten rode beside Naite, for Zani's marriage had made them brothers. To show good faith, Chodini also took his two wives and his youngest daughter.

Our chief went in trust; though he recalled how the Mexicans had poisoned the Hilaneh at Bavisco, these White Eyes were not Mexicans: they could not be so treacherous.

Chodini was no fool. When the White Eyes asked the warriors to yield their weapons before they ate, he retained a knife, concealed within his moccasin.

It was as well he did so.

The White Eyes' chief was no longer the hair-chinned man who had once sworn brotherhood, but a younger soldier whose face was burnt scarlet as a turkey's by the sun. Chodini and his family were invited to sit within a tent. Much food was spread on blankets. Chodini waited to see the White Eyes eat before any of his family partook of the feast. Then, taking meat from the same dish as the White Eyes' chief, he started to chew. All seemed well.

The White Eyes do not move silently, as do the Apache. Chodini had tasted but little when he heard the heavy-booted feet of many soldiers surround the tent. Laying down his food, angrily he demanded its meaning.

Blustering, the red-faced chief began to speak of a closed wagon that had been coming from the east. It had been attacked, its occupants killed.

"They were important people – a judge and his wife – not poor settlers. It will not be tolerated. You must pay for this attack."

Chodini had heard no word of such an incident.

Calmly he asked where this ambush had occurred. When the red-faced chief described the place of the attack, Chodini smiled, and explained patiently that this was in the territory of the Hilaneh Apache; the White Eyes should look to them if he wished for vengeance. He added, "But, my brother, you must know that the Hilaneh are a peaceful tribe. They are growers of corn and melons. To turn them warlike, the provocation must have been sore indeed. What hurts have been done to them by your people?"

The White Eyes' chief did not answer. He would not listen to reasoned talk. Peevish as a child, he slapped his hand upon the earth.

"You savages are nothing but liars! You and your men did this! You shall answer for your actions. You shall hang. We will have justice in this land."

It was then the red-faced man gave words of command. Around the tent came the sound of many guns being loaded.

The White-Eyed chief knew neither the speed nor the skill of an Apache. He had not moved from his place upon the ground before Chodini had slashed the skin of the tent and slipped through it. Ozheh followed. But now Red Face was screaming and laying hands upon Chodini's daughter, catching her by the hair so she could not escape with her father. The soldiers thrust their guns against the back of Naichise, and seized the arms of Naite and Huten and Parcohte and Chodini's wives as they tried to flee. Much noise was there as the troops fired upon the swiftly dodging Chodini and his son, but they reached the mountains without hurt.

Sickened to abandon his family thus, Chodini's face was grim indeed when he entered our camp. At once he gave orders that we move, for the soldiers knew where we were, and all were at risk from attack. Without question, and taking only what could be readily carried, we left our tepees and went higher into the mountains, up a precipitous trail that was easily defended from assault. We had scarce set foot amongst the rocks of the topmost peak when we saw black smoke rising as our tepees, our warm hides, the food we had gathered against the coming winter, were all put to the soldiers' flaming torches.

Only when darkness came did Chodini speak of what had happened in the White Eyes' tent. With cold, hard rage he told of the capture of his family.

By the firelight his warriors gathered.

In the grey light of dawn, we would ride against the White Eyes.

It was not a war party. Not yet.

We thought the White Eyes would take the family of our chief to Fort Andrews and hold them there. We could not attack the fort – it was too well protected – and even had we chanced it, we knew it would mean death for the captives.

"I will go forth alone and ask for their release," said Chodini.

"They will not grant it," said Golahka darkly. "The White Eyes will take you and then we will all be lost."

Chodini ground his fists into his temples in frustration. "These men are unreasoning! They are as wild as renegades! I do not understand their minds. How can we deal with such an enemy?"

As I sat staring into the flames, I saw the face of the woman settler who had snatched at her cake and clutched it to her chest. I saw the look of the Mexican who had died in defence of a cow. I saw the smallness of the White Eyes' souls.

"Possession is all to them," I said quietly. "Ownership. Trade. I think we must bargain with them."

Golahka caught my thought and pulled it into the light. "And to bargain, my chief, we must take captives of our own."

At the southern limit of the Black Mountain range a deep valley divides our territory from the mountains of the Dendhi, and through this pass the White

Eyes sent many carts and wagons to supply the forts that had grown upon our land. Full well we knew that Toah, chief of the Dendhi, and Sotchez, chief of the Chokenne, had once promised the White Eyes safe passage. But that was before the coming of the miners; before the soldiers made allies of the Mexicans; before the White Eyes' outrages upon our people had turned our friendship into enmity.

Leaving sufficient warriors to defend the tribe, we rode to the pass. There we concealed ourselves high in the rocks. There we waited.

After two sunrises, dust turned up by the wheels of a wagon appeared across the plain. It was driven by two men. Behind them rode five soldiers.

"Once more you bring good fortune, little sister," said Golahka. "We need but seven captives – one for each of our people – and here they are, steered towards us by the great hand of Ussen."

I started to smile at him, but he had turned away as if regretting that he had spoken. A pained spasm gripped me, as though Golahka had twisted his flint knife in my entrails.

All unknowing, the White Eyes rode into our ambush. Their horses were shot from beneath them. Outnumbered as they were, they made small fight back. Before long they were waving a white flag and begging mercy. An easy thing to grant, for dead they were of little use to us. They were bound by the wrists and driven before us, cringing, towards Fort Andrews.

Never had I seen men with so little dignity. They wept; they snivelled; they trembled like the leaves upon a tree. I was revolted by their cowardice. An Apache will look upon the face of death and meet its gaze full square. Had they no belief in the after-life? Did these men know no god, that they cowered so?

They were soft and could walk neither so far nor so swiftly even as an Apache child. To make the fort by sunset we at last sat them upon our horses, seven warriors – including Chodini – riding double behind them that they could not attempt to flee. My own horse was laden with the ammunition we had found upon the wagon, and so I too rode double with Golahka. Though I sat so close to him, the great distance between us remained. His face was shut tight against me, and for the whole of that long day he did not speak. Heart sore, I mourned the loss of his friendship. I knew not how to call it back.

We reached the fort as the light began to fade. Our party of warriors kept back, out of the range of the soldiers' shots. But Chodini, pushing his captive from his horse and leaving him for us to guard, rode forth alone and shouted for the White Eyes' chief to come out and talk. He would not do so. In terror, the blustering young man remained inside, calling down to Chodini from on high, ordering us as though we were a band of unruly boys.

"Go! Disperse from this place. Return to your homes!"

"The homes you have burnt?" Chodini answered. "How can we do so?"

The man paled. Even from that great distance I could sense his panic. A muttered consultation, a whispered word of command, and suddenly Chodini's two wives and youngest daughter were roughly pushed out of the gates. They knew the guns of our enemies were trained upon them and might at any time be fired, but still they walked proud, heads held high with the dignity of the Apache, across the great space to where the warriors waited. They reached us unharmed, and Chodini at once gave them horses and bade them ride swiftly to the high plateau where the rest of our tribe were camped.

Our chief was a just man. Watching the women ride to safety, he ordered the bands of three captives to be cut, and they were released. In screaming haste they fled, running towards the stronghold like rats to a hole. The gates did not open at once to admit them, and one man, whimpering with blind terror, tried desperately to climb the walls. In panic the soldier who stood on guard fired upon him, thinking this was an Apache leading an attack. The man fell dead upon the earth and there suddenly rose a great clamour of angry voices berating one another.

Chodini waited for the cries to cease, and then he called to the red-faced chief again.

"I have four more of your men here if you wish to fire upon them. A strange sport you White Eyes play! For my part, I would now have the rest of my family returned to me."

The red-faced man had been made to look foolish, and he now turned scarlet with high temper. Had his men not killed one of their own, he might perhaps have thought more clearly. I know not if there was a moment when war could have been avoided. But when he screamed at Chodini that his family would not be released – that they would face justice – he sealed his own fate. And ours.

Chodini rode – silent and grim – back to where we waited, and there on the plain beside the fort we made camp. Chee was there as a novice still, and he tended the horses without a word, before lighting fires to warm us and cook our food.

As I ate, I marvelled at the stricken faces of our

captives. They would not eat the dried meat we offered, but recoiled, sending the sour smell of their fear reeking through the night air.

Seeing my wonderment, Golahka at last broke his silence. "They have died a thousand deaths this day, have they not?" he said. "A brave man dies only once. It is certain that these White Eyes have no courage."

I was indeed perplexed. I did not fear to die, and yet full well I knew that there were other things I feared. I recalled the horror in the eyes of Denzhone after the Mexicans had shamed her. Did these men believe we would somehow hurt or dishonour them before death?

"Why should they dread us so? And, feeling thus, why do they enter our land and settle themselves upon it? None force them to come. And we surely did not invite them. Why do they not stay in their own land, where they belong?"

"I know not, Siki. I cannot comprehend their ways. But I feel we have an enemy here: one more deadly than the Mexican. For I have seen..." Golahka stopped and shrugged, finding no words to explain.

"From Ussen?" I asked, for I surmised that he too had been shown a vision.

Golahka nodded, frowning.

"I also." I spoke slowly, remembering the vision that Ussen had unrolled on the tepee wall. "I saw a monstrous child that stamped its foot and set our mountains shaking. A giant, yellow-haired creature that would not be satisfied, but must scream for more and more." I stopped. I did not speak of the dark-haired man who had beckoned the child forth, for Keste was dead. I could not speak his name.

Golahka looked at me piercingly. "We have seen the same, then. Would that I understood its meaning."

For some time neither of us spoke as we watched the flames leap in the darkness. So gladdened was I that I had his companionship once more, my face ached with the effort of self-control. In the warmth of the fire I felt the great chasm between us shrink and diminish until it was no more.

Smiling, Golahka clasped me by the shoulder. "Ah, Siki... Sometimes I would wish we had peace for many moons ahead..."

His voice was so soft, I dropped my gaze, for salt tears had begun to prick my eyes and I would not shame myself by weeping. When I raised my face, the chasm was there once more.

"We are warriors," Golahka said, his voice stripped of warmth. "It seems our fates are entwined in conflict. Sleep. At sunrise, there will be work to be done. We may yet see our brothers free."

But at sunrise all was lost.

At sunrise we saw the White Eyes' justice.

On the walls of the fort swayed the murdered bodies of our kinsmen. Naichise. Parcohte. Naite.

Huten.

They had been hanged, ropes looped around their necks, and left dangling until the life was choked from them.

With a wild, tormented cry, Chodini himself slew our captives: swiftly, cleanly, as becomes a warrior. Even so, they did not meet death with courage, but soiled themselves in abject fear before Chodini pulled his knife across their throats. The horror of his kinsmen's murder was compounded by their mutilation – for in this way they would enter the afterlife. Huten – that mild, sweet-tempered youth – would walk for ever with a stretched neck and blackly swollen tongue.

In revenge, Chodini tied the dead White Eyes by their ankles and dragged them behind his horse, galloping around the fort in fury, heedless of the shots that flew past him, that the White Eyes' chief might see what his actions had cost him.

For now Chodini made a fresh vow and one

which would not be broken: he would wipe the White Eyes from our land.

We rode once more to the pass; now no White Eyes would enter that place and leave it alive.

On Chodini's command, Golahka and I rode beyond it to seek the Dendhi and ask for their help; Ozheh went west to the Chokenne; Punte east, to the Hilaneh. Our women and children were camped high in the mountains. For now they were safe, but when the winter came, it would be cold and comfortless. If the White Eyes were still roaming the mountains by then, our people would become penned in like cattle. There they would starve. If we were to defeat the White Eyes, we must do so now.

I did not doubt that Sotchez and his warriors would follow Ozheh and join us on the warpath, for the blood ties between our two chiefs were strong, and Sotchez owed a great debt to Chodini for the freeing of the captives from Marispe. And the Hilaneh, already roused against the White Eyes, likewise would follow Punte. Chodini was not so certain that the Dendhi would take our part, as he knew well that their chief, Toah, had once promised safe passage to the White Eyes, and he might yet wish to keep the peace.

It was not until Toah called his warriors to council

that I learnt of his hatred of our enemy, and saw the injuries that had caused it.

The Dendhi were camped between the gently swelling hills. Trees ran down to where the broad river wound across the valley floor, and it was here that the tribe's tepees stood. As we rode into their settlement I felt a sudden, unmistakable chill of hatred and looked to see from whom it came. An old man stood glaring fiercely, his eyes fixed not on myself but on Golahka.

"There is one who loathes you," I said quietly. Stupidly. Had I thought, I would have guessed that this was the father of Tehineh.

"I know it," Golahka answered. "And I cannot blame him. If I had not made his daughter my wife she would yet be living."

Tehineh, who had ever been kind to me. Tehineh, who had loved me and called me little sister. Tehineh, whom I could not now recall without the fevered pain of jealousy clutching at my heart.

Toah came from his tepee to greet us, but said little. As his disfigured mouth often made speech difficult for him, words of welcome were instead spoken by his wife, Kaywin, sister to Golahka. She embraced him fondly, and then turned to me.

"You are Siki, the warrior? Much have I heard of

your prowess. Come sit beside me. We shall eat, and you must tell us why you come."

Scarce had we eaten on our ride from the Black Mountains, and we accepted Kaywin's food with pleasure.

Later, with full bellies, we sat amongst the Dendhi warriors at council. I saw but one face I knew well: Chico, from whose ears dangled ornaments of feather and turquoise – who had raced beside me, close as my own shadow, in our game of shinny. It seemed many moons indeed since we had camped victorious on that high plateau.

Golahka spoke first.

"I come once more to ask for help, not on my own behalf, but for my chief, who has been greatly wronged. The White Eyes have slain his brother and his brother's sons."

An angry outcry followed this news. It was a long time before Golahka could speak further.

"Chodini has made a vow to drive these intruders from our land. My kinsmen, will you join us?"

For a long time, there was naught but silence. Toah's eyes were lowered, and he gave his warriors no sign of his own feeling.

At last Chico said, "I am sorry for this great wrong. But the battle at Jujio cost many Dendhi lives. We still feel our losses."

Another warrior spoke. "I do not doubt the justice of your fight. But the insult was given to the Black Mountain tribe, not to our own. By you it should be resolved."

Murmurs of assent rippled through the Dendhi warriors. Golahka could do nothing but nod. He could not force them to fight. It seemed we must return to the pass alone.

It was then that Toah stood. I thought he would call the council to an end. But the Dendhi chief – so inflamed with passion that his words flowed with ease – began to speak.

"My brothers, before you make your decision, hear me. There is something you must consider before you answer Chodini's request. All know that lately I rode to the new-made settlement where the White Eyes dig for gold." Toah looked at myself and Golahka while he explained, "I went to talk with their chief, for there has been much trouble between our peoples, and I sought to bring an end to it." He addressed his warriors once more. "You know that he would not hear me, or listen to our just complaints. You know that he regards the Mexican, not the Apache, as his friend. But you do not know what more happened to me in that place, because until now I have been unable to speak of it. I have felt too ashamed; I did not wish to expose my humiliation before you, my brothers. But I speak of it now."

Toah pulled off the shirt that covered him and turned. Horrified gasps escaped from his warriors' mouths. His back was slashed – lacerated across its full width from shoulder to waist – with many deep wounds. There was silence as all waited for their chief to continue.

"Alone as I was, unarmed as I was, peaceful as I was, they laid hands upon me. They tied me to a post. They whipped me."

No angry clamour erupted at his words. In truth, Toah's warriors were too shocked to speak. No Apache would treat a dog thus. To do such a thing to a warrior was past imagining. To do it to a chief was unforgivable.

"Brothers, these creatures – I cannot call them men – have come upon our land and tear its flesh like vultures. While they remain we shall have no peace. You must do as you wish. But I shall join with Chodini in driving them from the face of Mother Earth. For me, that day cannot dawn too soon." Toah finished and, replacing his shirt, sat once more.

"I will come." It was Chico, his voice low, his eyes flashing with menace.

"And I."

"And I."

One by one the warriors agreed. No hesitation was there now.

So Golahka spoke of Chodini's plan. "Our warriors are at the pass. No White Eyes can now travel through it. Every wagon, every mule train, every stagecoach, is to be destroyed. Thus the soldiers will be drawn from the safety of their forts. We will do battle there, where the shape of the land gives us the advantage. There we will win."

Four sunrises hence, the warriors of the Apache nation gathered either side of the pass. Our force numbered near three hundred, but most remained hidden beyond the brow of the hills so that our enemy would not know our strength.

I was but newly made a warrior, and now I would have to prove myself. I stood beside my chief, ambushing and slaying the White Eyes that ventured through the pass. We gave no mercy, for we had been given none. And now I felt the value of the gun Golahka had set in my lap long ago. With this I could kill from a distance: I needed neither to look into the eyes of my enemy nor to feel their dying breath upon my face. I felt such loathing of those who came upon our land with contempt in their hearts that I was glad to keep far from them; I did not want to inhale their sour smell, touch their skin, see the stain of their blood.

For many days, we made attacks. But these were mere skirmishes; all waited for the time the troops would come, and the real battle would commence. They were slow to leave the safety of the fort, where even now the dangling bodies of our kinsmen were being picked clean by birds.

Only after one moon did the column of soldiers begin its reluctant march towards us.

At sunset my palms began to prick, and in the leaping flames of a campfire I saw the face of the White Eyes' chief.

"They come," I told Chodini. "The day that follows this. When the sun is high, they will be here."

Chodini nodded, and rose from the ground to spread word amongst the warriors.

The great ceremonial fire was built, and drummers split the night sky with the rhythm of war. As they sang – fierce angry chants that set my blood racing – warriors came out of the darkness and began to spin in the firelight. More and more joined them as their names were called. My own was shouted with a wild cry, and with an answering yell I joined them, dizzy with the rage and hot joy of battle.

But strangely, as I whirled, the buckskin strap

holding my quiver to my back snapped, and my arrows scattered upon the ground, falling at the feet of the spinning Golahka. He stopped, frowning, and the turning circle of dancers wheeled past us.

"Be glad it did not happen in battle," he said, bending to pick them up. It was then he saw the arrow that I kept wrapped and hidden, for its cover had come adrift. The blood drained from his face. He held it before me, and asked softly, "Your father's arrow?"

Mouth dry, I nodded. At that, Golahka gripped my arm and pulled me from the dance into the shadows where we might talk unseen.

"How came you by it?" he demanded.

"It was given to me," I replied. "By an old man of the Chokenne." I did not wish to say more, but Golahka's tone was full of quiet menace and would not be refused.

"Why did he give you this? Where did he find it?"

For a moment, I hung my head, but only for a moment. Was I not a warrior? I would not be cowed by Golahka. I was no traitor. That fault was my father's. Not mine. I lifted my chin high and answered, "He pulled it from the breast of my dead father." I met his eyes. "I know not who fired it."

Golahka's brow furrowed, and then his gaze slid from mine and rested upon the dark earth. He said nothing. Snapping the arrow in two, he walked silently from me.

But at last I had been given an answer to the question that had long festered within me.

Now I was certain. Golahka had killed my father.

How was I to cope with this knowledge? How was I to feel, having placed my heart at the feet of the man who had slain my father? My father, who had led his brothers into an ambush. Who had fled, and been killed for his cowardice.

I slept little, curled upon the ground with my hands balled into fists that I pressed against my eyes to stop the images that rippled across the lids. At the massacre of Koskineh ... at the battle of Jujio ... at the mine of Marispe ... in the search for Keste ... Golahka had always known of my father's treachery. Even as he agreed to train me he had known this betrayal was in my blood. No wonder, then, that he had watched so carefully for signs of it in me.

At sunrise we took our positions. The mass of our force remained hidden high on either side of the pass. But Chodini took his place low down, below the spring, where the thirsty soldiers would be drawn like cattle following their long, dusty ride. I went with him, as did Ozheh and Golahka. We would allow them to glimpse us; allow them to think there was but a small group of skirmishing Apache. When they came towards us, they would make a fine target for our warriors.

When the sun was overhead, Punte – who was scout – came swiftly to tell of their approach.

"Many soldiers, and two covered wagons. Their chief rides at the rear."

I shook my head, thinking how contemptible was this man, whose own actions had made us enemies, and who now drove his guiltless soldiers ahead of him to die.

Before long, we could see the clouds of dust thrown up by their horses' hooves, and I felt as though our warriors took a great inward breath together and then held still. It was as if the valley itself froze motionless, and waited.

The soldiers rode into the valley and gathered about the spring, allowing their horses to drink, and filling their own vessels with water. Chodini stood briefly, letting them see him before seeming to duck in hasty concealment behind a rock. Thus did Ozheh, and then Golahka. A simple ruse that an Apache child would not have believed. But the White Eyes took the bait. We were below them – they thought they had the advantage of the land. They bunched together and began to move towards us.

The rock Golahka had chosen to move behind was the one where I was already hidden. We crouched, side by side.

"The time is almost upon us." Golahka's breath was hot against my neck.

I must speak. "I am not my father," I said.

Lightly his fingers brushed my cheek. "Siki..." His voice was gentle. Tender. "I know it."

The heavy-booted tramp of many feet thudded on the living earth.

Our eyes met. "Fight well, little sister," he whispered, "but fight wisely. I would not have you enter the Happy Place yet."

"Nor I you," I answered.

A clasp of hands, and he was gone, for Chodini had fired his gun. The signal was given: our mass of warriors crested the hills. Low as I was in the valley, I could see how mighty a spectacle they made: many painted warriors on horseback outlined against the wide sky. The soldiers froze, aghast, for they knew themselves doomed.

Our great Apache force paused upon the hills, the victory to come already tasting sweet in their mouths. And then Toah gave a mighty shout that was echoed with a roar from the throats of the men who rode beside him. From the opposite hillside rang the answering cries of Sotchez and his band.

They sent their shots raining down upon our enemy and then rode in a glorious, sweeping charge down into the pass, encircling the White Eyes and cutting off their retreat.

Desire for blood burned hot within me, and from the cover of the low-lying rocks I fired, and loaded, and fired again at the soldiers. When my ammunition was all gone, I let my arrows fly forth into the breasts of these vile intruders.

Golahka had gone higher, and from there he fired with the skill and ease of a consummate warrior: not a single shot was wasted; each one found its mark.

Chodini watched for his quarry: he wanted the White Eyes' chief, for he would have revenge. But Red Face had climbed into a covered wagon and no doubt cowered there in terror, surrounded by soldiers who defended him. Many horses had been shot as our warriors charged, and the White Eyes used their bodies for cover as we did the rocks. Victory was ours – I felt the fist of the Apache almost close upon it – when from the covered wagon there came a sound I had never heard before. It was so loud that it sent the very air rushing from it in a solid wave that threw me onto my back.

When I stood, a terrible sight greeted me. Three warriors lay dead near by. Chico was one of them, his turquoise ornaments dripping with blood. They

were not slain with guns or swords, but torn apart
– limbs scattered – as though ripped to pieces by
some savage creature. Before I knew what had
happened, the sound came again, and I felt a great
blast hit the opposite side of the valley. I looked
at the White Eyes, for truly I knew not what had
caused this noise, unless it was the mountain spirits shouting their outrage. Perhaps Mother Earth
herself was roused to fury. I expected to see the
soldiers quaking in terror.

They were not.

Their wagons were covered no more. Red Face
stood, screaming at his soldiers. And already they
were loading once more: two giant guns that they
had fired upon my people.

Never had we seen such weapons. They could
not be fought. All knew at once the battle was lost.
And thus my brothers slipped away, riding swiftly
from that place and dividing into small bands.

On foot as I was, I too turned and fled. But as I
ran up the hillside, I stumbled and fell. I tripped not
over rock, but over a body.

Golahka.

He breathed still.

The great gun had hit the very rock he hid
behind, sending a huge shard of stone crashing

down upon his head and rendering him senseless. He bled from a wound that gaped wide, showing the gleaming skull within. There was no time to bind it. I had to run. Hide. But I could not leave him there for the soldiers. We were yet hidden from their gaze. My eyes searched swiftly for shelter.

There! A slab of rock fallen across two low boulders. A space beneath. I dragged Golahka to the place, folding his uncooperative limbs and wedging him tight into the gap. Scraping at the earth, I scattered handfuls of dust upon him to conceal his shape, rolling a large stone to rest before him. Scarce had I covered our tracks, and rubbed earth on my own skin and in my hair, before I heard the heavy tread of the White Eyes' boots. I moved quickly to the other side of the slab and crawled in beside Golahka.

I shut my eyes too late against the horror that followed. I saw what they did. And in the long, cold nights that came afterwards, I wished with all my heart that I could wipe their butchery from my mind.

They took knives and, laughing, cut at the bodies of my dead brothers. They took trophies of flesh. And now my kinsmen walked the spirit world without hair. Without noses. Without ears. If the Apache became savage in the coming years as the White

Eyes said, then it was these men that taught it us, for I had never seen anyone scalped until then.

One came, whistling, his feet crunching upon the fallen rock. He sat on the slab above me, his monstrous boots swinging but a finger's width from my face, and, striking a match against the rock, proceeded to smoke a pipe. I moved not, for well I knew that the smallest flicker would tell him of our presence. I felt the body of Golahka tense beside me, and knew he had come back to his mind. Apache as he was, he remained still, but my relief that he lived was so strong that I was certain I had set the air about me quivering like the rising heat from the desert plains.

But the White Eyes have no feeling for living things. The man was no more aware of me than of the rock he sat upon. When his chief gave commands, he stood. He folded the bloodied ears of Chico – the ornaments still dangling from them – within a white cloth and slipped them inside his pocket. Still whistling, he went on his way. Soldiers were being sent into the mountains of the Dendhi to search for our people. I could not see them, but I doubted not that others were being sent into our own Black Mountain range.

I watched the departing backs of the White Eyes, and suddenly my stomach heaved within me.

For amongst those many men, with their heads of grass-yellow hair, walked one whose hair was black. He was as dark as a Mexican. Or an Apache.

Red Face squatted in the valley like a vast toad, his great guns either side of him to fire on any Apache that showed themselves. We could not cross to our own mountains, yet neither could we flee into the hills of the Dendhi behind us lest we come upon the many soldiers we had seen enter there.

Thus, at nightfall, Golahka and I moved west, skirting through the lowlands before turning for the south, where we hoped to find safety. Golahka spoke not a word of complaint, though he was sorely injured and dizzy from much loss of blood. Scraping thorns from the leaf of a prickly pear, I pulled the sides of the wound together and bound them beneath the split leaf as I had with Dahtet. As I did so I saw the skull was crushed, and I trembled at the sight of it.

On foot, we travelled dangerously slow. Full well I knew we must have a horse, if we were to get far enough from the pass to avoid the soldiers. And yet how was I to find one? But the White Eyes had multiplied on our land like the rabbits on the upland plain. Rising before me in the clear moonlight was the smoke of a settlement.

It was a sign of his great hurt that Golahka made no protest when I told him to rest where he was. He lay upon the ground and I went forth alone.

Many cattle were penned in a wide corral, and amongst them ran a number of horses. I needed but one. One might pass unnoticed; one would not provoke pursuit. A sturdy mare stood at the edge of the herd, grazing quietly. She was stocky and would carry two with ease. And she was no showy riding horse that would soon be missed. I had no rope, so I untied the cloth that bound my hair, and crept softly into the corral.

Had their dogs barked, had the horses startled, all would have been lost. But they did not. I watched the mare until she saw me, and then turned my back and crouched low in the dust, trusting that her curiosity would bring her to me. When she nudged my shoulder I twisted so that I could blow breath into her nostrils. Her trust settled upon me, and gently I tied my strip of cloth around her muzzle so that I could lead her away. Slipping the poles of the corral down, I took her out, replacing them as soon as she was freed, for I wished to delay the discovery of her loss. From the animals' trough I filled my vessel; I did not know when we would next find water.

Golahka did not spring upon her back, but rather mounted as a small child will do, by digging the toes of his moccasin into the skin above her elbow and using the horse's bone to aid him. He sat awkwardly, his back curving to one side, and I knew that if we rode swiftly, as I wished to, he would be unseated. Mounting behind him, I turned the horse's head away from the Black Mountains, away from where the soldiers' fires burned brightly in the darkness.

All that night I scarce knew where we rode. The sky was clouded, and I could see no stars. Without the moon, neither could I see the line of distant mountains to guide me. I was truly lost.

At dawn, I did not recognize where we were, but of one thing I was certain.

We were followed.

It was the pricking of my palms that told me. The pricking of my palms, and a chill that sent the flesh of my arms into small bumps.

Leaving Golahka to rest and eat what little meat we had, and setting the horse to graze, I crawled to the crest of a hill.

Many soldiers.

A dark-haired man.

They were yet far from us, and they were on foot, but across that great distance I could see that they had picked up our trail. The dark one looked in our direction, his eyes shaded by his hand.

I knew not what to do. If we went by foot we would be harder to follow. But Golahka could not walk far: they would swiftly catch up with us. Thus we moved on, taking no rest, no sleep. Golahka I forced to remain on the horse, while I walked behind, sweeping our tracks away with brushwood as best I could. I thought to get into Mexico, for although it was the land of our enemy, it was not the land of the White Eyes. The Mexican guards what he considers his territory with a jealous fervour. I hoped the White Eyes would not dare pursue us there.

Through that long day, we edged southwards, and each time we paused, I knew the soldiers drew ever closer. My palms began to burn with their nearness. Late in the afternoon I climbed a tree, and saw that the dark-haired man was now ahead of the White Eyes. He came on alone. At great speed. His tracking never failed, no matter how I tried to mislead him with false trails.

Golahka had taken himself to the place where he felt nothing as a means to drive away his pain. All that day, he had not spoken. But when he saw my troubled expression he returned to me.

"Tell me, Siki," he said, his face braced tight against the hurt he now felt. "They come nearer?"

"There is one whose hair is black. He comes ahead."

"A scout. A good one. He tracks as well as an Apache."

I did not wish to doubt my chief, but I could not help it. "Did you see Keste die?"

"I did not." Golahka's tone was flat. "No more did Chodini. We trusted his father." His eyes were bright with challenge once more. "Were we wrong to do so?"

I did not answer his question, but said, "We must move on. Could we but get to Mexico we may be safe."

Golahka laughed. "Strange, to seek refuge in the land of our enemy! But these days are strange, are they not, Siki?"

"Indeed."

There was nothing more to be said. We went on, on, on, until our mouths were dry, our tongues swollen, and the horse near to dropping. We had not reached the Mexican border, and I knew we would not do so before we were caught. Golahka's eyes had clouded, and my hands were scalding with the closeness of the man who trailed us, when at last I saw a single juniper tree, clinging to a rock.

Keste's valley. A hidden place. If it were Keste that followed, he would know of it. Yet it had but one entrance. Easily defended. We could go nowhere but there.

Golahka dismounted and edged stiffly beneath the rock that was the doorway to the hidden valley. Not troubling now to conceal her hoof prints, I slapped the mare across the rump and sent her galloping away that she would lead our pursuer behind her. Walking on stones so as not to leave a trail, I too slipped beneath the rock.

I could see at once why Dahtet had thought it akin to entering the Happy Place. Bushes hung with berries, and sweet water flowed.

We drank. We ate.

We waited.

And before long, a soft scrabbling informed us that our pursuer still followed. A great chill set my teeth chattering. It was Keste, I was certain. Who but Keste would know of it?

With the last of his strength, Golahka stood, pulling the knife from his waist. As the man's dark head appeared, Golahka seized his hair and, yanking his head back, put the knife to his throat.

When I saw his eyes I screamed in horror.

The dark-haired man was not Keste.

It was my father.

Still holding his hair, Golahka lowered the knife from my father's throat and twisted his head to face him.

"Ashteh." Golahka's tone was flat, heavy, as if unsurprised. "We thought you dead."

He released his hold and my father stood upright, displaying his White-Eyed garb, unperturbed by the scrutiny of the great warrior.

"Ashteh is dead, as you see." He smiled, his easy charm oozing forth. He spoke Apache, but his phrasing sounded strange to my ears, stilted, like that of the White Eyes. He spoke with no trace of shame. "They call me John Bridger."

I had not heard his voice for many, many moons. It was as if I had been bitten by the savage wind of winter: it chilled me to the bone. I felt the dead walked once more upon the living earth. Or perhaps my fleshly being had slipped into the afterlife and now roamed amongst the spirits – unhappy, tormented ghosts for ever scarred by mutilation.

"John Bridger?" Golahka laughed with contempt and shook his head. "I see there is a tale to be told, but I have no wish to hear it. John Bridger... Do you not know your daughter?"

My father turned. Those eyes fixed on me in disbelief. Astounded, he sought the child in my woman's face. And then he gasped with shock. "Siki?" he asked. "My little Siki? You have become a warrior?"

My tongue lay leaden in my mouth. I recoiled,

flinching, from his gaze and did not answer. My father heeded not, but spoke once more.

"I see it is so! By God, fate is a curious thing! Who could have wagered that the child of a Mexican would become an Apache warrior!"

Mexican?

My father was Mexican!

The fragments Ussen had shown me took their true shape. At last I saw the whole. Mexican. Taken as a child. Reared by the Chokenne as their own.

Horror threatened to sweep me away. Feverishly, I whispered, "Only half my blood is yours."

"That's true," my father replied. "But your mother too was taken as a child. Oh, Siki... Did you never wonder that you had so few relatives amongst the tribe?"

He was indeed a ghost: an evil spirit whose cold, dead hand reached inside me and pulled my innards upwards through my throat. With that one speech he deprived me of all. In one stroke he cleft me from my chief; my tribe; my self.

I could not speak. Could not act. Could do nothing.

The wounded Golahka spoke for me. "The soldiers will soon be upon us. Will you give away our hideout, John Bridger? For I warn you, we will fight, and your daughter is a fine warrior. I doubt you will win this battle."

My father hesitated. Then he shook his head. "I will go," he said hoarsely. "I will tell them the trail is cold." He took one last look at me, a desperate plea in the familiar eyes. "Come to me, daughter, I beg you. These past years I have longed to speak with you. I will be at Fort Andrews. Find me there."

And he was gone.

Golahka sat down heavily, leaning against a rock, his breath drawn in slow, pained gasps. Sickened with shame, I sank to the grass at his feet, hot tears spilling down my face. I could not stop them falling.

With immense tenderness, Golahka placed his hand beneath my chin and raised my face to his. "Siki," he said softly. "This matters not. The treachery is not yours."

My tears ran freely over his fingers. Aghast at my foolishness, I whispered, "I thought him dead! I thought you had killed him!"

Golahka's eyes narrowed. "And was this the reason for your great silence?" he asked.

I nodded. "I thought you watched for my own betrayal."

Golahka laughed, in pain though he was, with seeming relief. "Siki, when I watched you it was not for that!"

"You knew he lived?"

"No. I knew he fled. But I thought him slain in the ambush. So did we all. Then, when we returned from Jujio, I saw a man slip inside a tent as we approached the White Eyes' camp. I thought it was him, but had only the merest glimpse. I could not be sure."

"I saw a dark-haired man there too. But I never thought it could be my father! Why did you not speak of it?"

"Because you did not. You thought him dead. When we danced before the battle you spoke of it with such certainty. How could I tell you otherwise?" With his tear-wet hand, he stroked the hair away from my face. "Truly, Siki, I have had such delight in you! I have known such fierce joy in your company. I could say nothing that would cause you pain. Did you not know why I watched you? Could you not see?"

I looked at Golahka in confusion. My father had torn the heart from me; I scarce knew what he said.

"I am Mexican." It sounded within me as the clanging of the bell upon the house of their tortured god.

Mexican.

Enemy to Golahka.

Enemy to my people.

The wild cry of an abandoned child rose within

295

my chest. "Why did my mother not tell me?"

"Why? Because it was of no importance!" Golahka said fiercely. "It matters not!" He held my face. "Blood is nothing. Nothing! Would Ussen whisper to one whose spirit was not Apache? Your soul is Black Mountain, and your heart too. Can you not feel it?"

Winding his hands in my hair, he pulled me to him and held me still, until I felt his heartbeat answering my own.

"We have the same heart, Siki," he whispered, his breath warm in my hair. "The same soul. We have grown from the same earth, you and I. Our roots entwine in the living rock. Hold fast to that certainty. It is the only truth that matters."

So it was that in the gathering dark of that hidden valley, I became wife to Golahka.

By dawn I was his widow.

Golahka's arm was cold across my back, his fingers wound, unmoving, in my hair. I lay upon his chest. No heartbeat replied to mine. I knew him dead, and yet for a long time I did not stir. I could not. I pressed my warm body against his as if by doing so I could give him life. I longed to vanish into him like the melting snow. I wanted nothing but to follow him into the Happy Place.

But flesh is not so obliging. It makes its own demands and forces the body to endure. To go on. To survive no matter if the spirit within has died.

I left him there, twining saplings around and above him into a wickiup shelter, for I could not bear to dig a hole and cover his beloved face with earth. Leaving him lying on the sweet grass, I went from the valley.

I walked towards the Black Mountains, for where else could I go? I came quickly upon the horse I had sent galloping. Perhaps she had not fled far, or perhaps my father had caught her and brought her back, for I was certain that it was he who had hobbled her beside the flowing stream. She had grazed and rested and stepped out eagerly when I climbed upon her back.

I rode unwarily, taking no care for concealment. With every step I invited death to come. But my life, it seemed, was a small, worthless thing, for neither man nor beast would take it. Neither did Ussen want my spirit, for he sent small game scurrying across my path. My well-trained warrior's body killed and ate without ever any conscious thought passing through my sorrow-deadened mind.

At dawn on the sixth day, I entered the Black Mountains. By sunset I came into our camp on the cold peak. The gaunt faces of my tribe watched me, warmed for a moment with the light of hope.

"Golahka comes?" asked Chodini.

I did not speak. I did not even shake my head. My eyes met those of my chief. In one look I told all.

As word of the great warrior's death passed from mouth to mouth, all hope was extinguished. Despair settled heavy with the darkness, and death wails echoed across the mountains.

I made no sound. My cry was trapped within me.

I slid from the mare's back and stumbled. A gentle touch steadied my elbow and I turned. Dahtet took me by the hand as her eyes spilt tears. Without a word she led me to her brushwood shelter, and wrapped me in her own blanket. She fed me with the meagre broth that boiled upon her fire. And for that long night, and the many nights that followed, she lay warm against my back, holding me as I had once held Tazhi.

It was the hardest winter my tribe had ever endured. Chodini took warriors into Mexico, but returned empty-handed, for although he had captured many beef, the White Eyes had robbed him of them, and returned them to the Mexican. Pressed as we were between these two enemies, our people began slowly to starve.

I told Chodini of my father. He was little surprised to hear Ashteh lived, for he too had glimpsed the man who hid within the tent.

"I see it pains you, daughter," he said. "But your blood is of no consequence to me."

I should have rejoiced that Chodini took so little heed of my father's treachery. But I could find comfort in nothing. Nobody. When I looked at the faces of my tribe, I saw strangers. I could not hold fast to certainty as Golahka had urged me, for without him, there was none. And it was bitter indeed to know that he walked in the Happy Place beside Tehineh while I remained on the alien earth alone.

When Chodini set forth to raid once more, I did not go with him. I would be naught but a hindrance and a danger to him. For to fight well a warrior must lust to live, and with each breath, I wished to die.

In Chodini's absence, Dahtet's child was born – a son – whom she held with fervent passion. The infant cried ceaselessly. There was not enough to feed Dahtet, and so her son hungered too. I went alone to hunt such small game as I could find, for I sorrowed to hear the child's cries. Often I returned empty-handed; everywhere I went it seemed the White Eyes had stripped the land of all that moved upon it. Sometimes I came home with rabbits, birds, mountain rats. By the time such meat was divided amongst the hungry, there was barely a mouthful for Dahtet. Yet we survived, clinging to life by our fingertips, my living heart weighing like a stone within me.

Through that long winter our camp smelt of defeat: it soured the air and poisoned all who breathed it. It was not only the battle at the pass that caused this despair, for in truth we had survived such losses before; it was the vision that Ussen spread upon the night sky that told the tribe it was vanquished.

When Chodini returned again from Mexico he brought but one stringy mule to feed near three hundred of his tribe. Two warriors had been lost in gaining even this, for he had been pursued by soldiers of both the Mexican and the White Eyes' army.

It was midwinter. At Chodini's request the medicine man built a ceremonial fire, scattering herbs upon it. As the scented smoke rose skywards, our great chief chanted prayers to Ussen, for sorely were his people in need of guidance. In answer, Ussen painted a picture on the moonlit clouds.

Marching across the night sky were many soldiers, all dressed in the same dark uniform. Men whose hair was yellow, and whose skin glowed pale. They marched side by side together, a hundred – a thousand – abreast, faces devoid of expression, looking neither left nor right. Could there be so many men upon the living earth? I stared, thinking that soon they would stop; they must stop. But no end was there in sight. The men marched shoulder to shoulder, until the vast dome of the sky was filled with their number; and yet still more came over the horizon to push them forward.

And my father's face appeared large on the clouds. He smiled to the White Eyes and beckoned. He led them towards the mountains, and they swarmed upon the land, over the sweet grass and the living rock, until the entire body of Mother Earth was covered.

The Apache nation was no more.

And as I watched this vision unfold, I knew the worst of horrors – that I had sought to avoid since Tazhi had been slain – was now upon me.

I carried Golahka's child.

A child I could not protect from these invaders. A child I could not keep safe. A child who – if it remained Apache – was as helpless and as doomed as the rest of the tribe.

Two sunrises after Ussen showed us this vision, Chodini called his warriors to council. In the cold morning light, our chief looked aged and beaten.

"Brothers," he said, his voice heavy with weariness, "we cannot live thus. I cannot sit idle and watch my people starve. I will go to the White Eyes to ask for peace."

An outcry followed this speech. Ozheh, son of Chodini, spoke fervent words of protest. "My father, you cannot go! Have you not seen the White Eyes' justice? You think they will let you live?"

"I am chief. I will do all I can for my people."

"You think your death will aid us?"

"It may serve what they think is justice."

"You shall not go!" Ozheh said with passion.

"I must," answered Chodini. "And should I not return... If the council agrees, you, Ozheh, will become chief in my place."

When Chodini set forth, he was not alone. I went with him.

"Your father can serve as interpreter," said Chodini bleakly. "Perhaps this way the White Eyes' chief will better understand my words."

I had no desire to see my father; all curiosity had died with Golahka. But I could not refuse my chief's request. Long since had we eaten our horses, and so, reduced to beggars, we would walk to plead with the White Eyes.

Ozheh took me aside before we departed. "They will not grant peace. Can you not see this?"

"I do not go to talk with them; I go at my chief's request. I do what I must. As do you."

Ozheh gnawed his lip and said no more. He embraced Chodini as though he wished to hold him there in the mountains, and in his eyes I saw Ozheh's knowledge that he would not see his father again.

They laid hands upon us. Of course they did. We had scarce stepped within the gates of the fort before they stripped us of our weapons and bound us by the wrists. They did not wait to hear my chief's plea, but forced us towards a barred room where we would not see the sky.

Imprisonment.

Unendurable.

Ahead of me, Chodini's stride broke. The soldier nearest him jabbed savagely at his ribs, and he turned in irritation.

A cry of rage. A single shot. Silence.

My chief lay dead.

And the wail that had been trapped within me burst from my throat like the anguished howl of a wounded beast. A soldier pointed his gun at my heart; I was within a hair's breadth of entering the Happy Place. Joyfully would I have done so. But my cry had alerted my father to my presence. Before I could move and provoke the soldier to fire upon me, Ashteh appeared, shouting words of the White Eyes' tongue.

I little heeded the exchange that followed. I knew only that the soldier put down his gun. The bands that bound my wrists were cut, and I was given over to my father. It seemed he had told Red Face that I was his child – a captive of the Apache – who now wished to return to my own people. With this lie, he bought my life.

I did not want it.

I watched them drag away the body of my chief, knowing well they would take knives and cut trophies from his corpse. Contented, wiping his hands, Red Face walked from that place. His men went back to their tasks.

Desolate, I knelt in the dust. Return to my own people? Who were they? For what had made me Apache? Love of Golahka. Love of my chief. Both gone, what had I left? I looked at the future and saw nothing.

Into my wretchedness, my father gave an awkward cough, and then spoke. "Tell me, Siki, your mother – is she well? Has she taken another husband?"

I could do naught but laugh – a high, fevered gasp. "My mother? My mother is dead! Mexicans slaughtered her."

His eyes at once filled with tears. Tears that

flowed as easily as mine had done for the dog killed at the end of its rope.

Fury filled me. "My brother too." I spoke without mercy; I wished to wound, to slash through his easy sentiment and bring him pain. "Yes – I had a brother. Your son. Slain as a child – hacked down by Mexicans."

His tears dried; his face paled. My words pierced him. Now he felt a small fragment of the anguished whole.

"If you are Mexican," I said, "you are my enemy."

"No." Crouching on the earth before me, my father lowered his face to mine. "Siki, listen to me. You are not Apache."

As he said this, my anger deserted me. He spoke truth. I felt weak as Dahtet's babe. Enemy blood filled my veins. I would have cut my vessels and let it spill upon the soil, but I had not weapons for even this simple task.

My father began to talk. "Siki... Listen to my story, then you may judge. Know all that has happened before you set yourself against me."

I recalled Golahka's words to him: *I see there is a tale to be told, but I have no wish to hear it.* No more did I. But I lacked the strength to stop the stream of words that swirled about and began to drown me in their sweetness.

"You know of the ambush, I think? On that journey – my last as a warrior – we passed by the very house I had been stolen from as a child. I remembered it. I saw the face of my mother; I recalled her death. Suddenly I knew myself to be Mexican! I was so startled by it, I knew not what to think. I was cleft from my self, or so I felt. I could scarcely contain the cry that burned in my throat. When I was sent forward to scout I walked carelessly, heedlessly, my mind full of troubled thoughts.

"I didn't see the troops until they sprang their ambush. I had led the warriors into a canyon; we were an easy target. For this, I knew I would be blamed. And then I found I could not fight! Every Mexican face seemed to be that of my father, my mother. I stood motionless for what felt like hours. Days. Potro began to shout at me to fight, to be a man. And still I could do nothing. I fled. I suppose Potro thought I had led them there deliberately and so pursued me. He intended to kill me, Siki, as a traitor, a coward."

Ashteh's eyes dropped to the ground. Dull was his voice as he confessed, "I am no Apache, Siki. I was terrified to die. And so I killed Potro.

"He lay dead at my feet, and I stood there, knowing that now I could never return to the Black

306

Mountains. Yet neither could I be a Mexican, for how could I ride against my wife? My child?

"The terrible sounds of the battle were distant by then, and after that came silence. I could see more troops approaching, and I guessed that any Apache who survived would not stay to bury the dead. I knew Potro's body would not long be recognizable – the coyotes would see to that. And so I did a desperate thing. I hung my amulet about his neck. If anyone found him later, they would think it was I who had been killed. Ashteh died then."

"Did you never think how it would seem that your corpse was pierced by your own arrow?" I said flatly.

My father sighed, shaking his head. "Truly, Siki, I believe I ran mad for a while. For many months I knew not what I did; I knew not who I was. Often I thought of you and your mother. But you were safe. I was an exile. And I did not want you to be without a tribe, without a people, without a name, as I then was.

"Eventually I went east, and found the white man! They saved me. They have fashioned a new world. Such buildings they have made, Siki! Such wealth ... such splendour. Do you know they have houses as tall as trees! And I have heard that in some you can turn a piece of metal, and heated water will gush from a spout!"

"Is your soul so small it can be bought with a vessel of hot water?" I asked.

He laughed, knowing no shame, and continued eagerly, his eyes glistening with boyish excitement. "It is a new nation, Siki. A fine one. And now I am neither Mexican nor Apache. I am American. In this new world, I am reborn as John Bridger."

I said nothing, but I thought of Keste: fashioning his own tribe where he might shine with glory. I had been right in thinking Ashteh was like to him.

My father placed his hands on my shoulders. His black eyes gazed, unblinking, into mine, holding me still, unmoving, as they had in the pine tree at Koskineh. I knew then that Ussen had not only shown me glimpses of his past: the visions I had seen had been a warning of my father's future.

He spoke with quiet fervour. "Know the Apache are doomed, Siki. The Americans will have their land, and nothing can be done to stop it. I have seen what has happened to the tribes in the east. Believe me, the Apache are powerless against the American might. There are thousands of white men – you cannot imagine how many – and more come every day. Will you not join us? You are a warrior. Choose the winning side!"

His honeyed words flowed, glinting as alluringly as the golden tears of the sun that sparkle in the mountain stream.

I was exhausted by the weight of grief I carried. How much more could be loaded upon me before I broke like a dried-out twig? I must bring word of Chodini's death to his starved, despairing people. To Ozheh. To his wives, his children. Hear their wailing cries. I baulked at the task.

The great circle of hatred and vengeance and bloodshed turned and turned, and I could not stop it.

But I could perhaps step beyond its reach.

Clasping my head in my hands, I felt the lure. To go from conflict. To end the fight. To cease to struggle with every breath. I thought of the child within me. Was it not to this babe that I owed my loyalty now? Should not my whole being go to protecting this new life? Could I truly find a place where the child could grow? Where I could watch it play without daily fear of its slaughter?

It was temptation indeed.

I yielded.

But not before I asked, "Why did you not stay in the east? Why did you help the White Eyes against those who were once your brothers?"

My father could not meet my eyes. It was a long time before he answered.

"A man must live. I was paid to come here, Siki. And I hoped to find you and your mother and save you from the conflict to come." He lowered his voice as though ashamed of his next words. "Besides ... the land called me."

The land.

Ussen's land.

The earth: my mother.

Since the death of Golahka, my spirit had lain heavy, seeming dead within me. But now – even as the leaf buds burst forth in spring – it unfurled. Fresh. Vibrant. Strengthened by its sleep.

The land.

There was more here than Golahka or my chief. The wind in the trees, the wide sky above my head, the sweet grass beneath my feet. The earth, the rocks that knew me. The land, whose beating heart was the Apache. Here I must live, or die. Only here, upon this soil. For ripped from this earth I would wither and perish as surely as the tree that is torn from its roots.

I belonged to this land. As did the child that grew in my belly. To this certainty I held fast.

I rose from the dust. I gazed up at the sky, and drew in a breath of the clear air. Looking towards the fort gates, I said, "I will go back."

My father gasped. "Siki! That way lies disaster."

"I know it."

"You will be pursued. Hounded. Persecuted without mercy. Hunted like the deer."

"It matters not."

"Siki … daughter…" My father's voice was both desperate and uncertain. "You will die!"

"As must all men. As must you. But I will die proud. I will die free. And first I will live, and I will fight. I am Apache."

Historical Note

This is a work of fiction, based on events that took place on the border between Arizona and Mexico in the second half of the nineteenth century. It was inspired by the autobiography of Geronimo (edited by S. M. Barrett), and the first-hand accounts that were collected by Eve Ball in *Indeh: An Apache Odyssey* and *In the Days of Victorio: Recollections of a Warm Springs Apache*. I'm deeply indebted to those of the Chiricahua Apache nation who spoke to Eve Ball and allowed her to publish their stories.

Some incidents in the book are based on real events: there was a massacre of Apache who had gone south to trade, and a subsequent battle to avenge their deaths. Apache women and children were captured and enslaved by Mexicans and then freed by warriors when their captors entered a church to worship. Apache land was invaded and stolen from them by white settlers.

However, each of the tribes, all of the characters and every place name are fictional. I've made no attempt to produce an accurate historical novel: this is an imagined evocation of how it may have felt to have lived through events like these. I've tried to be authentic as far as period detail goes, but at times I have had to stretch things in order to make the story work. If there are mistakes, I apologize.

T.L.

Acknowledgements

On a personal note, I'd like to thank my children, Isaac and Jack, who for several months had a mother whose mind was almost entirely in Arizona; my husband, Rod Burnett; my mother, Wendy Brown; and Louise Griffiths for reading the first draft with enthusiasm; Lindsey Fraser for tireless encouragement; Louise Rands Silva for cups of tea and moral support; Eugenio Navarro and Nestor for helping me get the Spanish right; Rob Harvey for advice on natural history; Averil Whitehouse at Walker Books, my editor of exceptional talent; and, finally, Leland Michael Darrow, tribal historian, Fort Sill Apache tribe, Oklahoma, whose notes and comments on the text were invaluable.

About the Cover Photograph

This portrait of Hattie Tom, a Chiricahua Apache woman, was taken in 1899 by American artist, Frank Albert Rinehart. Commissioned to photograph the 1898 Trans-Mississippi and International Exposition in Omaha, an event which brought together Apache tribes from across the American Midwest, Rinehart and his assistant, Adolph Muhr, spent two years photographing Native Americans and their way of life. It was during this time that they captured this image.

Very little is known about Hattie Tom. Born in 1886, the year her parents Chiricahua Tom and Coshey, a White Mountain Apache, were imprisoned, she grew up as a prisoner of war. She married Clement Nahgodleda, a grandson of the great chief Cochise. Both died in 1901.

About the Author

Tanya Landman was inspired to write *Apache* by a chance remark about warriors. She says, "The image of a girl carrying a spear formed behind my eyes, but I didn't know if a Native American woman would have been allowed to become a warrior." Tanya began researching and found references to Lozen, a female warrior. "The more I read, the more I found that what I'd imagined was entirely plausible."

Tanya Landman is the author of many books for children including *The Goldsmith's Daughter*, her second book for teenagers. Since 1992, she has been part of Storybox Theatre, working as a writer, administrator and performer – a job which has taken her to festivals all over the world. She lives with her family in Devon.

You can find out more about Tanya and her books by visiting her website at www.tanyalandman.com

Bibliography

Primary sources

Ball, Eve (with Nora Henn and Lynda A.
Sánchez): *Indeh: An Apache Odyssey*
(University of Oklahoma Press, 1988)

Ball, Eve: *In the Days of Victorio: Recollections
of a Warm Springs Apache*
(University of Arizona Press, 2003)

Barrett, S. M.: *Geronimo: His Own Story*
(Leo Cooper Ltd, 1975)

Betzinez, Jason (with Wilbur Sturtevant Nye):
I Fought with Geronimo
(University of Nebraska Press, 1987)

Miller, Lee: *From the Heart: Voices of the
American Indian* (Pimlico, 1997)

Opler, Morris Edward: *An Apache Life-Way:*
The Economic, Social, and Religious Institutions
of the Chiricahua Indians
(University of Nebraska Press, 1996)

Roberts, David: *Once They Moved Like the Wind:*
Cochise, Geronimo and the Apache Wars
(Pimlico, 1998)

Additional sources

Basso, Keith H.: *Wisdom Sits in Places: Landscape*
and Language Among the Western Apache
(University of New Mexico Press, 2002)

Brown, Dee: *Bury My Heart at Wounded Knee:*
An Indian History of the American West
(Vintage, 1991)

Debo, Angie: *A History of the Indians of the*
United States (Pimlico, 1995)

Debo, Angie: *Geronimo: The Man, His Time,*
His Place (Pimlico, 2005)

Goodwin, Grenville and Basso, Keith H.:
Western Apache Raiding and Warfare
(University of Arizona Press, 2004)

McChristian, Douglas C.: *Fort Bowie, Arizona:*
Combat Post of the Southwest, 1858–1894
(University of Oklahoma Press, 2005)

Robinson, Sherry: *Apache Voices: Their
  Stories of Survival as Told to Eve Ball*
  (University of New Mexico Press, 2000)

Stockel, H. Henrietta: *Women of the Apache
  Nation: Voices of Truth*
  (University of Nevada Press, 1991)

Thrapp, Dan L.: *The Conquest of Apacheria*
  (University of Oklahoma Press, 1988)